Christmas at Darcy House

A Pride and Prejudice Variation

Victoria Kincaid

ISBN: 978-0-9997333-0-1

Chapter One

"Bingley!" Darcy called out, quickening his step to catch up to his friend. "Bingley!"

Bingley slowed as he glanced over his shoulder. "Darcy?"

Darcy chuckled. "I have been calling your name for minutes!"

Bingley shook his hand when Darcy reached him. "I beg your pardon. I suppose my thoughts were elsewhere."

"I was on my way to Bingley House to collect you for a bit of riding if you have the taste for it."

A tepid smile spread over the other man's face. "That would be just the thing. Exercise is precisely what I require to put me in spirits." His friend had been out of spirits too frequently of late, Darcy had noticed. Since their return from Hertfordshire in November, he had grown quieter, almost melancholy.

"Excellent!" Darcy perhaps did not require as much distraction as Bingley, but he had also felt a little out of sorts since returning from Hertfordshire—although there was no obvious reason. Perhaps a ride would help him dispatch some of this restlessness. "Shall we start off from Darcy House?"

"Yes, but I am not attired for a ride," Bingley said. "Would you accompany me to Bingley House so I may change my clothing?"

Darcy managed a wary smile. "Certainly." With any luck, Caroline Bingley would be away from home, and Darcy would not need to exchange pleasantries with her.

As they traversed the remaining distance to Bingley House, the two men conversed about the weather and mutual acquaintances. When Bingley opened the door to his home, however, Darcy's hopes of escaping the man's sister were immediately dashed.

Miss Bingley's nasal voice blared into the hallway from the adjoining drawing room, although it was impossible to discern the words.

"Dash it all!" Bingley exclaimed. "Caroline and Louisa have guests. If I do not say hello, they will give me no end of grief about it."

Darcy sighed. It would be the height of bad manners not to accompany his host in to greet his sisters and whatever guests had arrived. "Of course."

The drawing room was inhabited by women, who all rose and curtsied when the men entered. Darcy and Bingley both bowed. Darcy first noticed Bingley's sisters, Louisa Hurst and Caroline Bingley. The third woman was a bit older and unknown to him. The fourth woman…

The fourth woman was Elizabeth Bennet.

By some sort of alchemy, the sight of her instantly extracted all the air from his lungs. His breathing ceased altogether, and it was possible his heart stopped beating as well. He knew, somewhere in the dim recesses of his mind, that a civil greeting was called for. But the entire English language appeared to have deserted him.

Fortunately, Bingley was not stricken with the same affliction. "Miss Bennet!" he cried, a broad smile on his face. "I did not know you were in London!" *Good Lord*, Darcy thought. *If Bingley were a puppy, he would lick her face.*

"I arrived but three days ago," Elizabeth replied with a smile that was far more reserved. "I am in London to celebrate the Christmas season with my aunt and uncle." She gestured to the older woman. "This is my aunt, Madeline Gardiner."

"I am delighted to make your acquaintance," Bingley said. Darcy gave her a nod as she repeated the sentiment. She was not ill-favored and was dressed in a very genteel manner, quite different from the garish costumes Elizabeth's mother and younger sisters favored.

"The Gardiner family lives on Gracechurch Street, in *Cheapside*," Miss Bingley drawled. Mrs. Gardiner flushed, and Elizabeth's expression darkened. Had the entire conversation been like this? If so, Darcy was amazed they had not drawn knives already.

"Tell me," Bingley hastily addressed Elizabeth, "did you arrive in London alone? Did not Ja—any of your sisters accompany you?"

A flash in Elizabeth's eyes showed she had noticed Bingley's slip. "Unfortunately, I am quite alone. Jane was to have accompanied me, but she had a fall the day before and was unable to come."

"A fall!" The alarm on Bingley's face suggested he was prepared to ride for Longbourn that instant.

Elizabeth's intent scrutiny of Bingley was at odds with the light tone of her voice. "Nothing of great import. She slipped on the stairs and sprained an ankle, but the apothecary wants her to stay off her feet for a week or so. She was sorry to miss the chance to visit."

Bingley's face had gone quite pale. "Please give her my best wishes for a quick recovery." Elizabeth nodded.

"How distressing!" Miss Bingley exclaimed. "I hope it will not hinder her fine dancing."

Mrs. Hurst snickered. Jane Bennet was not terribly light on her feet, and the Netherfield drawing room had witnessed many derisive comments to that effect.

Elizabeth eyed the two women narrowly. "I should not think so. She is always sought as a dancing partner."

That was true, Darcy reflected. The woman was quite pretty and had an amiable temperament; he believed she had not sat out one dance in the time he was in Hertfordshire.

Bingley bounced on his feet, again resembling a restless puppy. "I pray you, give her—er, your family—my regards."

"I shall," Elizabeth promised with a knowing smile. *If only her eyes would sparkle at me like that! Although then it would be impossible not to kiss her. And the curls curving around her neck...*

"Shall I also give them *your* regards?" After a moment Darcy realized Elizabeth addressed him, an impish smile on her face—teasing him once more.

"By all means," he replied.

The women seated themselves again. Bingley hovered anxiously near the doorway, and Darcy with him. Now would be the perfect time for the men to take their leave, but Bingley obviously wished to stay and learn more about the happenings in Hertfordshire.

Ordinarily Darcy would have been eager to continue with their plans, but Elizabeth Bennet's fine eyes drew his gaze like a lodestone. Over the past month he had convinced himself that he had exaggerated her beauty in his memory. That distance and separation would lessen his ardor for the woman. Now he was dismayed to discover he was wrong.

Bingley inquired about a mutual acquaintance. Elizabeth replied, and a conversation was engaged that required the two men to take seats in the drawing room. Miss Bingley made a sour face—she was eager to separate her brother from any of the Bennet family—but Darcy could not have been more pleased.

Elizabeth's dark curls, her delicate lips, her light and pleasing figure—everything about her was as uniformly charming as always. Not only could Darcy fail to remove his eyes from her person, but he also found himself wishing she would occasionally glance at him instead of Bingley.

Naturally, she is looking at Bingley; they are conversing about events in Hertfordshire, and she would like to secure him for her sister.

But this awareness did not help to dispel Darcy's disquiet over her persistent attentions to his friend.

Evidently Miss Bingley was also discomfited by the conversation, for she inserted herself into it rather abruptly. "How fortunate you are, Miss Bennet, to be in London during Christmastide. It is delightful. December in Hertfordshire, I would imagine, is rather…brown."

Elizabeth blinked. Between one moment and the next anger glinted in her eyes. Miss Bingley remained oblivious, but Darcy recognized the danger.

"Is that why your party departed from Netherfield so suddenly?" Elizabeth asked in a deceptively innocent tone. "It was excessively brown for your tastes?"

Bingley had already given his sister a quelling glare over her snide tone; now he hastened to respond. "No. Of course not! I-I simply had pressing business back here in town."

Elizabeth pursed her lips. "I hope it was concluded satisfactorily?"

Bingley relaxed into his chair, believing the disaster averted. "It was."

Oh no. Bingley cannot see the trap she laid for him. "Then we shall expect the pleasure of your company back at Netherfield soon?" Bingley appeared to choke on his tongue, and his sister's face turned an unbecoming shade of purple.

She knows. She knows there was something behind our departure beyond the all-purpose excuse of "business." Darcy should be chagrined that his party had been caught being less than correct. He should be appalled that Elizabeth was drawing attention to it.

Instead, he experienced an obscure sense of pride. In effect, she had forced Bingley to admit they had lied, twisting the knife effortlessly. Even Caroline Bingley could not best Elizabeth at this game.

Out of loyalty to Bingley—not to mention his own sense of self-preservation—Darcy should not have focused so much attention on Elizabeth Bennet. However, his eyes had too long been starved for the sight of her face; it was like drinking water after a long trek in the desert.

Miss Bingley had recovered a modicum of her composure. "You would not have us leave town at Christmastide, would you?"

"I understood most families preferred to be in the country at Christmas," Elizabeth remarked with wide, seemingly innocent eyes.

Darcy experienced a sudden fit of coughing. Elizabeth was quite correct. London at yuletide was not fashionable, although enough families of the *ton* remained to create some society. The Bingleys no doubt would have preferred Netherfield, if not for the desire to separate Bingley from Jane Bennet.

"London has its pleasures as well at this time of year," Miss Bingley said through gritted teeth. "There are...er...mummers, and clowns at the Drury Lane Theatre, and Astley's Amphitheatre has a special Christmas show."

Miss Bingley could not possibly intend to partake in any of those entertainments. Such low-brow delights were entirely beneath her notice.

"And we have been invited to any number of balls and dinners and card parties," she concluded with a sniff to remind Elizabeth Bennet that *she* had not been invited to such events.

"How lovely," Elizabeth responded brightly. "No doubt you shall pass a happy Christmastide here. Many consider the company in Hertfordshire to be quite *confined* and *unvarying*."

Oh, that was a shot across Darcy's bow. Her mother had taken exception when Darcy used that phrase to describe Hertfordshire. Elizabeth shot him a sly look, perhaps daring him to object, but he did not even frown at her. Instead, he was too busy suppressing a grin.

"That is not why—We did not leave because—! I found Netherfield, indeed all of Hertfordshire, quite charming," Bingley insisted earnestly. "I am eagerly anticipating my return, even if my sisters choose not to accompany me."

Miss Bingley narrowed her eyes at her brother but did not respond.

"We would be quite happy to see you there!" Elizabeth exclaimed. "Although, of course, we would miss your sisters exceedingly." Her tone implied the opposite. "But my whole family would be quite pleased, Mr. Bingley." Was she deliberately leaving Darcy out of this oblique invitation? *No. I am being overly sensitive. She is simply making a point to Bingley's sisters.*

"And what about you, Mr. Darcy?" Miss Bingley inquired. "No doubt you and Georgiana shall be departing for Pemberley ere long."

Darcy had not, in fact, decided where they would pass Christmastide. Georgiana had hoped they would stay in London since some of her friends were remaining, but in general he preferred Pemberley during the holidays. London could be bleak and dirty. However, it could offer one thing that Pemberley could not: Elizabeth Bennet.

"We will be remaining in London," Darcy heard himself say.

Miss Bingley's eyebrows shot upward. "Indeed? It will be lovely to have you here." But her eyes darted from him to Elizabeth; maybe she suspected the other women's influence on his decision.

Mrs. Gardiner cleared her throat. "Lizzy, perhaps we should depart. We have other calls to make."

"Of course." Elizabeth stood gracefully, a tiny smile playing about her lips. Evidently the strain in the conversation had not bothered her.

Darcy made a point to bid Elizabeth goodbye but could think of nothing more to say to her. She was always so witty, so at ease in company—and he was always so tongue-tied in her presence.

The door closed behind the two women. "Well!" Miss Bingley exclaimed. "I shall not feel myself obliged to return Miss Bennet's call!"

"I rather believe she will not mind," Bingley said, sinking disconsolately into a chair. Darcy considered this. Bingley's sisters believed Elizabeth had visited Bingley House to curry favor with them and perhaps secure introductions to the *ton*. However, Elizabeth's behavior belied such an aim.

But why had she bothered to visit Bingley's sisters at all? Her visit had merely served to make Bingley and his sisters feel uncomfortable about their hasty departure from Hertfordshire.

Oh.

Darcy considered the other inhabitants of the drawing room. Mrs. Hurst's brows were drawn together in an expression of perplexity. Miss Bingley drummed her fingers on the arm of the chair in irritation. Standing at the sideboard, Bingley had poured himself a glass of brandy and now stared into the empty glass.

Elizabeth was angry at the way they had departed from Netherfield and suspected it had been for the purpose of separating Jane Bennet from Bingley. Perhaps Miss Bennet had been more attached to Darcy's friend than he had supposed. Certainly *Bingley* was dejected after their separation. The observation made Darcy uneasy; had he done his friend a disservice?

And did Elizabeth suspect Darcy's role in the relocation to London? The thought made him grow cold. She had not given Darcy any particular regard during the conversation, but surely she had noticed his interest in her.

Still, the thought that Elizabeth Bennet was angry with him persisted at the back of his mind. How would he know for sure? And what could he do about it?

Not that he wanted to, he reminded himself. *Elizabeth Bennet is nothing to me.*

Chapter Two

Caroline Bingley lingered at the back of the book shop, regarding the clock with some impatience. Twelve minutes past the hour, and he was late. Did he have no sense of punctuality? Not that she expected anything else. Although she professed to love books, in truth she found bookshops dreadfully dull. However, they were a far more convenient location for a hidden rendezvous than a mantua maker's or a milliner's shop.

The bell over the door rang as someone entered, and Caroline averted her eyes to shelves of natural history books in which she had no interest. Quick footsteps warned that someone was approaching. "Miss Bingley! What a pleasant surprise," a low, male voice said.

Caroline turned around with a completely feigned expression of shocked delight on her face. "Mr. Wickham. How lovely to see you," she said softly, scanning the area to see if they might be overheard. But the shop was sparsely populated, and nobody was within earshot.

He curled a lip at her. "Enough with the act," he growled. "What do you want with me? And how will you make it worth my while?"

Caroline pursed her lips, determined not to surrender to the temptation to display her real thoughts about the man. "I have need of some assistance and will pay you handsomely for it."

Mr. Wickham leaned closer; his breath smelled like old onions. "Do tell."

When Caroline had encountered Wickham on the streets of Meryton in October, he had offered her "inside knowledge" about Mr. Darcy's habits. She had disdained him then, never expecting to want his help, but today's business required just his sort of cunning. "Miss Elizabeth Bennet is in town, staying with relatives in Cheapside," Caroline explained. "I have an…interest in ensuring that Mr. Darcy does not become…overly fond of her."

Mr. Wickham arched an eyebrow. "He has an inclination in that direction? She hardly seems high enough in the instep for him."

Caroline wished she could forget the expression on Mr. Darcy's face as he had gazed at Elizabeth Bennet the previous day. "I do not see the appeal," she sneered. "But he appears to be in danger of falling under her spell."

Wickham shrugged. "And how is this my concern?"

She glanced down at her gloves, soft and white, without a spot of dirt. "As I recall, in Hertfordshire, Eliza Bennet seemed to have some misguided fondness for you." Caroline did not bother to hide her expression of disgust, but he did not react. "Have you continued the acquaintance here?"

"I have paid calls at her aunt and uncle's house," he allowed.

Excellent. Caroline's plan might work. "I will pay you handsomely to ensure that she is no longer a suitable object for Mr. Darcy's affections."

The man stroked his chin, feigning perplexity. "And how should I accomplish that?"

"Propose marriage to her," Caroline said promptly.

Wickham's mouth turned down in disgust. "I do not wish to wed her!"

Caroline rolled her eyes. Must she do all the thinking? "You need not actually marry her. It is sufficient to make her an offer. Once she is engaged, Mr. Darcy's interest will wane."

"And might turn in another direction?" Wickham regarded her shrewdly from under his brows.

"That is not your concern," Caroline informed him frostily. "I merely wish to have her removed from consideration temporarily."

"I do not know…" Wickham examined his fingernails with studied indifference. "It seems a great deal of trouble for me…."

Caroline recognized her cue. She extracted a small pouch from her reticule and handed it to him. He opened it immediately—how gauche—and allowed the coins to spill out onto the palm of his hand.

"I trust that is sufficient incentive," Caroline said.

Avarice glowed in his face. "Indeed. I believe I can feel my affection for Miss Bennet increasing by the second."

"Excellent," Caroline said. "I will leave the matter in your hands."

Wickham smiled at her wolfishly. "A pleasure doing business with you."

***

The knowledge that Elizabeth Bennet was in London had not allowed Darcy a moment's rest that night. As he sat behind his desk that evening, he envisioned what she might be doing. Perhaps she was having dinner with her aunt and uncle. Now she might be sitting in the drawing room reading. Did they have children for her to play with? When would she retire for the night?

After brooding in his study until long after midnight, he had tossed and turned in his bed before falling into a fitful sleep in the early morning hours. A mere ten minutes in her presence, and he was in danger of becoming as obsessed with her as he ever was.

Upon awakening, his first thought was that he knew where Elizabeth stayed; he could call upon her and the Gardiners. Indeed, a visit was polite—nearly obligatory—given his acquaintance with her family. She had been gracious enough to call on the Bingleys despite knowing that she would receive a frosty welcome, but the Bingley sisters plainly would not return the call. If Darcy visited, at least Elizabeth would know that the entirety of the Netherfield party did not hold her in such low esteem. Also, she might have been brought low by the Bingley sisters' insults; it was only right that Darcy visit and ensure that she was in good spirits.

Given new life by these thoughts, Darcy sprang from bed and addressed himself to his toilette with dispatch. In the midst of splashing water on his face, he had a new thought. *If I visit the Gardiners' house alone, will I appear to be courting Elizabeth?* He had taken great pains in Hertfordshire to avoid the appearance of favoring her; he did not want to give rise to expectations he could not fulfill.

And yet his own reaction surprised him. The idea of creating such an expectation should fill him with dread, but instead a thrumming excitement surged through his veins. Suddenly light-headed, Darcy grabbed the edge of the washstand. Was there some part of him that wished Elizabeth to believe he was courting her? Or worse yet, *wished* to court her?

Darcy regarded his own rather pale face in the mirror. What could he do?

He pried his gaze from the mirror and stumbled to the closet in search of fresh clothing. *I am being foolish.* He was simply returning a social call for the sake of politeness. Elizabeth would understand that he only visited because of his connection with her family. He might happen to enjoy Elizabeth's company…quite a bit…more than any other woman he had ever encountered…

But that was beside the point. His object was to help her feel welcome in London.

As his valet entered the room, Darcy thrust such thoughts from his mind. Within minutes he was dressed and downstairs breaking his fast.

Another half an hour saw him driving his curricle toward Gracechurch Street. The curricle was a bit of an indulgence; it would have been simpler to take a horse. But he had a vision of offering Elizabeth a chance to tour some of his favorite sights in London. It was a ridiculous thought, yet Darcy found he could not dismiss it from his mind.

Guiding the curricle through the streets of London, he even found himself humming a tune that Georgiana had played the day before. It was pleasant to have one of his Hertfordshire acquaintances in London. There was nothing remarkable if the anticipation of her company pleased him.

The Gardiners' home was not large, but it was well kept and more fashionable than Darcy had expected. He had never ventured into Cheapside before and had been prepared for far less genteel surroundings. This appeared to be a quite respectable neighborhood.

Darcy was still humming as he approached the Gardiners' door and knocked. Perhaps he should have purchased flowers. Women liked flowers, did they not? But flowers might suggest he was courting her, which he most definitely was not. They were simply friends.

A maid answered the door and took his coat. Darcy gave his card and inquired if Miss Bennet and Mrs. Gardiner were at home. The maid replied that they were in the drawing room with a male visitor whose name she had not caught.

Darcy's interest was immediately piqued. He could not imagine Elizabeth had a large circle of acquaintances in London. Could she have acquired a suitor already? But the maid had not mentioned the age of the visitor. He might just as easily be some friend of her father's or a business acquaintance of her uncle's. Darcy frowned at the thought. A widower of that age might prefer a younger wife.

Or perhaps it was Bingley, visiting to apologize for his sisters' behavior the previous day. Yes, Bingley would be quite acceptable.

Darcy followed the maid down the narrow hallway to the drawing room. She opened the door and announced, "Mr. Darcy, ma'am," before withdrawing and allowing Darcy to enter the room.

His eyes immediately fell upon the male visitor, and he realized he had been far from imagining the worst.

Wickham.

His arrival had interrupted a scene of some mirth. Wickham was grinning while Elizabeth giggled, and Mrs. Gardiner had her hand over her mouth as if to suppress laughter. When Darcy stepped into the room, the merriment quickly died away.

The other man raised his eyes slowly to meet Darcy's, a smirk forming on his lips. "Darcy," he drawled.

"Wickham." Darcy bit off the word.

Everyone stood to exchange an awkward series of bows and curtsies. Darcy seated himself in the closest available chair, which happened to be opposite Wickham's. Unfortunately, the other man was also adjacent to the settee where Elizabeth and her aunt were situated. *How did Wickham come to be in London? Why was he visiting Elizabeth? Was he actively courting her?* Darcy's breakfast sat like a lump of lead in his stomach.

He could not forget Elizabeth's disappointment that Wickham had not attended the Netherfield Ball and her spirited defense of him during the dancing. The conversation had caused Darcy twinges of anxiety, but he had comforted himself that her meager dowry kept her safe from Wickham's depredations. In perpetual want of money, the man would never pursue a poor woman.

And yet here he was.

"I was not aware you were in town," Darcy said pointedly.

Wickham gave him a lazy smile. "I have a fortnight's leave for Christmas and thought I would visit some friends here in London." *In other words, he was in town to gamble.* "I would not have expected to see *you* in Gracechurch Street."

Darcy stiffened. "I am on good terms with the Bennet family," he said sharply. "And I made Mrs. Gardiner's acquaintance yesterday."

"This is my third visit," Wickham smirked. "The Gardiners are most charming hosts."

Three visits already? Perhaps he *was* courting Elizabeth. The room was too warm and too close. Sweat dampened the back of Darcy's cravat, and he tugged to loosen it. It was unfair that providence had gifted Wickham with such pleasing manners and easy ways with people. He readily formed friendships while Darcy struggled simply to say appropriate words in social situations.

Mrs. Gardiner cleared her throat. "Mr. Wickham and I both spent our childhoods near Lambton, in Derbyshire."

Darcy suppressed a desire to shout that he knew very well where Lambton was.

"We have many acquaintances in common," she continued. Darcy no doubt had acquaintances in common with Mrs. Gardiner as well; unfortunately, they most likely took the form of having patronized the shops that members of her family operated. *How have I arrived at this pass?* His feelings for Elizabeth had brought him so low that he was beginning to regret his superior birth.

"I grew up at Pemberley," Darcy said.

The older woman's eyes grew wide. "Oh...Darcy! I should have realized—!" She turned to her niece. "You neglected to inform me that the Mr. Darcy of your acquaintance was Mr. Darcy of Pemberley!"

Elizabeth's expression revealed no chagrin. "I did not realize you would know the name, Aunt."

So she had rarely discussed Darcy with her aunt, and yet Wickham arrived for frequent visits. Darcy had the distinct impression he was losing a footrace he had not known he was running.

For the rest of the visit, Darcy remained an outsider. Elizabeth knew how Wickham liked his tea. Mrs. Gardiner inquired after his cousin's health. Wickham referred to incidents which had occurred at Longbourn after Darcy had left for London.

Darcy made only occasional forays into the conversation, but his subjects were not taken up by the others. In desperation, he blurted out an invitation for Elizabeth to join him for a curricle ride through London.

She blinked at him, a faint line forming between her brows. "I thank you for your most generous offer, Mr. Darcy. But I fear I might be contracting a cold and do not believe it would be prudent for me to remain outside for great lengths of time."

"Of course," Darcy murmured while Wickham smirked. "Another time perhaps."

Nevertheless, Darcy refused to quit the drawing room and leave Wickham in possession of the battlefield. To do so would not only admit defeat but would also leave Elizabeth unprotected from the other man's whims. As a result, both men stayed quite a bit longer than was customary. Finally, Mrs. Gardiner announced she felt a headache developing; both Darcy and Wickham regarded that as an invitation to depart.

Darcy preceded Wickham out of the door but did not mount his curricle. Instead, as the other man exited the house, Darcy caught him by the elbow and hissed in his ear. "Lovely day for a walk. Shall we?" With a jerk of his arm, he forced Wickham along the footpath beside the road.

"Whatever is the matter, Darcy?" Wickham grinned lazily. "Are you feeling neglected?"

Darcy's free hand curled into a fist, but he forced it to remain at his side. "What are you playing at with Elizabeth Bennet?"

"Playing at?" Wickham said with affected innocence. "I enjoy her company."

"So you *are* courting her," Darcy said from behind clenched teeth.

"What is it to you if I am?"

Stopping abruptly, Darcy spun the other man about to face him. "She has no dowry to speak of. You could not possibly be interested in more than a dalliance."

Wickham put his hand to his heart. "Do you think me so mercenary as all that, Darcy? I am insulted, sir!"

Darcy's patience had worn out. He held Wickham in place with a hand on his shoulder and stared fiercely into the other man's eyes. "If you hurt her—or her family—in any way, I will make sure you suffer for it."

"I have the greatest admiration for Miss Bennet and have no intention of harming her." The sincerity of his words was belied by his noxious smirk.

Darcy shook the other man by the shoulder. "I am not making an idle threat."

Wickham shrugged. "I have debts, Darcy. I may be forced to flee London. If I do so, I might prefer some company." He winked.

Darcy's fist raised, but he managed not to strike the other man. *How can he think such despicable things about Elizabeth? How can he be so disgustingly cavalier about her virtue?* "She would never join you," he hissed.

Wickham eyed Darcy sardonically. "If you say so… Then you have no cause for anxiety." He flung off Darcy's arm. "I suppose time will tell." After flashing Darcy a knowing grin, the other man hurried away. Darcy did not stop him.

He stood in the pathway, clenching and unclenching his fists, trying to get his ragged breathing under control. *Damnation! I have tipped my hand. Wickham is not stupid.* The officer recognized Darcy's interest in Elizabeth.

But Wickham's presence at the Gardiners' had taken Darcy by surprise. The officer was more than capable of continuing to pursue Elizabeth just to spite Darcy. Wickham had no true feelings for her, and he had no intention of proposing marriage, but his presence could impede Darcy's plans with Elizabeth.

Not that I have any such plans, of course. I am simply being friendly.

Still, how could he protect Elizabeth from Wickham? Darcy envisioned various schemes involving bodyguards or Bow Street Runners watching the Gardiners' house, but they were impractical and unlikely to succeed without Elizabeth's cooperation.

There was nothing for it, he concluded reluctantly. He must tell Elizabeth why Wickham was unsuitable company. Hesitant to spread gossip and unaware of which lies Wickham had told Elizabeth, Darcy had refrained from speaking of the matter before. But now it appeared to be the only way to protect her.

Chapter Three

Elizabeth stood on her tiptoes to scan the ballroom, wishing she were taller. The Marlowes' ball was quite a crush, and it was difficult to discern individuals on the other side of the room. The ballroom itself was beautifully decorated, festooned with gold and deep red ribbons as well as swags of pine branches and holly. Mistletoe seemed to adorn every doorway and corner. She would have to be careful not to be caught under a bunch lest some man importune her for a kiss.

Frustrated with her inability to see, Elizabeth climbed up a few steps to a landing, which provided access to the French doors opening onto the terrace. Of course, it was December, so the doors were tightly closed. Aunt Gardiner followed her up the steps. "Perchance are you seeking a particular young officer?"

Elizabeth blushed and said nothing. She had been disappointed when Mr. Wickham had not attended the ball at Netherfield in November. However, he had told Elizabeth he was acquainted with the Marlowe family—who seemed to know everybody in London—so she had every reason to hope he would be present for this occasion. While Elizabeth was not like Kitty and Lydia, chasing after every man in a red coat, she would not mind seeing the dashing figure of Mr. Wickham in his regimentals, and it would not be a chore to stand up with him.

"He is an amiable, well-spoken young man," Aunt Gardiner continued. "Your uncle and I quite enjoy his company."

"It is pleasant to have an acquaintance from Meryton here in London," Elizabeth replied. While she had not precisely been missing Hertfordshire, she had been somewhat overwhelmed by the constant stream of new acquaintances since arriving in town. She must have met everyone her aunt and uncle knew in London, including the Marlowes, whose fortune derived from a firm that did business with her Uncle Gardiner.

Mr. Wickham was always a welcome sight. Mr. Darcy, on the other hand, was not. It was so unfortunate that he had arrived only a few minutes into Mr. Wickham's visit yesterday. Elizabeth had been anticipating a pleasant conversation with Mr. Wickham—and perhaps a walk in the nearby park. But Mr. Darcy's arrival had created a scene of great awkwardness.

Elizabeth had hoped Mr. Darcy's antipathy for the other man would compel him to quit the Gardiners' house quickly; instead he had remained, scowling and unpleasant, until Mr. Wickham took his leave. The man had already stolen the living bequeathed by Mr. Darcy's father. Must he deprive the poor officer of good company as well? Mr. Wickham had borne it all with great equanimity, but Elizabeth had discerned signs of strain on his countenance.

Unfortunately, Mr. Darcy would be attending the Marlowes' ball as well. When Elizabeth had arrived with the Gardiners, their hostess had been breathless with excitement over the news. "Mr. Darcy of Pemberley! He had initially informed us that he would not attend, but this morning we received a missive that his plans had been altered, and he would be able to grace us with his presence. Such a coup! It is well known he so rarely accepts invitations to any occasion. But perhaps"—Mrs. Marlowe had flicked open her fan and employed it vigorously—"he has heard tales about our fine balls. Everyone enjoys them. They are always much talked about! I would not be surprised...." She lowered her voice to a whisper. "To discover he altered his plans specifically so he would not miss it."

"That must be the case, madam," Elizabeth had responded. "He certainly is not attending so he can see me!" Mrs. Marlowe had laughed at her joke.

Elizabeth endeavored not to dwell on Mr. Darcy's presence and consoled herself that he was unlikely to seek her out. He had performed his duty to their acquaintance by calling on the Gardiners—and plainly had little joy in it. No doubt he had many other friends he would prefer to see.

At that moment Elizabeth spied Mr. Wickham. He was on the other side of the vast room, speaking with a petite blonde woman; but when he happened to glance in her direction, Elizabeth caught his eye. He answered with a broad smile—he really was quite handsome—and proceeded to plough through the crowd in her direction.

Her attention was drawn from him when her aunt tugged her arm. Following her aunt's gaze, Elizabeth saw, to her horror, that Mr. Darcy was also wading through the crush of people in her direction. His eyes were intent on her the way a wolf's might be when stalking a doe.

Whoever arrived first could claim the next dance with her. "What shall I do?" she asked her aunt. "I have no desire to dance with him!"

Her aunt nodded. Mr. Darcy's cold manner the day before had not impressed her either. "I know, my dear. But you cannot refuse him unless you are prepared to refuse all the young men at the ball."

Elizabeth knew this, of course; it would be disgracefully rude to refuse one man and accept another. She glanced at Mr. Wickham; he was closer than before, but not as close as Mr. Darcy. Mr. Wickham glared at the other man and tried to move more quickly, but the crowds would not give way. *I beg you to hurry!* she importuned him silently and then cast an eye about the room for a means of escape. But the crush of revelers was so thick that she could not easily evade Mr. Darcy's approach. *Why does he even wish to dance with me? He does not enjoy my company!*

The bizarre footrace continued for a minute until—unfortunately— Mr. Darcy arrived, scowling and dark-eyed. He climbed the steps to the landing, a little out of breath. "Miss Bennet, would you do me the honor of the next dance?" he puffed.

Mr. Wickham emerged from the crowd, red-faced and sweaty. His mouth twisted in a grimace as he climbed the steps.

Elizabeth gritted her teeth. "It would be my pleasure, Mr. Darcy."

She immediately turned her attention to Mr. Wickham, who smiled and bowed ingratiatingly. "I see I have arrived too late for this set," he said lightly. "But perhaps you would agree to partner me for the following set?"

Elizabeth smiled at him. "Yes. I thank you, Mr. Wickham."

Mr. Wickham immediately disappeared into the crowd; Elizabeth did not blame him for eschewing the other man's vicinity. But Mr. Darcy stayed by her side, a looming and taciturn presence, awaiting the beginning of the next set. *Why in the world does he wish to dance with me when he evinces no interest in my company?* Elizabeth chatted with her aunt, who shot many curious glances in Mr. Darcy's direction.

Finally, the previous set's dancers drifted away. Mr. Darcy took Elizabeth's hand to lead her down the stairs and into position for the next set. There were a great many couples dancing, and Elizabeth had much leisure time to converse with her partner. Unfortunately, her partner did not appear interested in conversation, even once the dancing commenced.

After a minute or two of silence, Elizabeth had grown quite annoyed. "Mr. Darcy," she said finally, "since you and I have not been in company for above five minutes, I am at a loss to understand how I have already incurred your displeasure."

His eyes grew wide. "Miss Bennet, I assure you that you have done nothing to displease me."

Was a scowl his natural expression, then? "*Something* must have displeased you," she replied. "For I do not believe I have ever seen anyone scowl so frequently while dancing." She softened her words with a pert smile.

His head jerked backward. Was there truly nobody in his life who would speak to the man with any degree of sportiveness? It seemed altogether foreign to him.

The steps of the dance drew them apart, but when they were reunited, he said, "I assure you that any displeasure I might experience does not fall to you." Ah, it must be that Mr. Wickham's presence disturbed him. *I could ask him about it, but we have already had one contentious conversation on that subject.*

Mr. Darcy continued, "I was quite pleased to discover you would be in attendance tonight."

Quite pleased? Elizabeth rather doubted that, but she made allowances for the way a man usually complimented a woman. How had he known in advance she would be at the ball?

"I will endeavor not to scowl for your sake," Mr. Darcy said and managed a smile. It was a forced and ghastly thing.

Elizabeth laughed. "I believe, sir, that I prefer the scowl. It fits more naturally on your countenance."

She had expected him to laugh or shrug off her teasing, but instead his face lost animation and he cast his eyes downward. Or was that her imagination? After a moment he said, "I see I must practice my smiling for your sake."

"Do not inconvenience yourself on my account," she retorted.

His eyes caught and held hers. "Your pleasure is never my inconvenience."

Elizabeth swallowed, unable to look away. There was a moment of electricity between them, as if the air that separated them could burst into flames. A similar jolt of energy had occurred as they danced at the Netherfield Ball. How odd.

They were obliged to separate again and partner with the dancers adjacent to them. When they were returned to each other, Elizabeth made an inquiry after the Bingley family's health, and the remainder of their conversation was quite civil and dull.

At the conclusion of the set, Mr. Darcy led Elizabeth toward the refreshment table and gently inquired if she would care for a glass of punch. A bit astonished that Mr. Darcy had not fled her vicinity at the first opportunity, Elizabeth replied in the affirmative. While he was fetching the punch, she took advantage of his absence to seek out Mr.

Wickham. However, she could not distinguish him at all, which perplexed her greatly. The next set was beginning to form, and she expected he would come to claim her as a partner as promised.

Mr. Darcy returned with the punch, and she thanked him, drinking thirstily. Then he inquired whether she would like to cool herself with a visit to the terrace. Elizabeth blinked rapidly. Why did he wish to spend more time with her when he gained so little pleasure from it? "I promised this set to Mr. Wickham," she said, casting her eye about the room once more.

Mr. Darcy grimaced. "Apparently he has…forgotten." He gestured toward the dancers where Mr. Wickham was partnering the young blonde woman he had been speaking with before.

Nonplussed, Elizabeth stared for a long moment. After competing so eagerly for the chance to dance with her, why would Mr. Wickham then abandon her? Mr. Darcy regarded her with something like pity in his eyes. "Wickham's attentions are ever fickle. Would you accompany me for a turn about the terrace? There is a matter of some urgency I must discuss with you."

His darkly intent stare was most disconcerting, sending shivers racing along her spine. But she had no reason to refuse the request, and she was feeling more charitably inclined to him; at least he had not abandoned her to dance with someone else. Indeed, it was flattering that Mr. Darcy appeared not to have an interest in any of the other women at the ball.

Mr. Darcy offered his arm, and they climbed the steps to the French doors that opened onto the terrace. At the first blast of cold air, Elizabeth was reminded that it was indeed December. But she had grown overheated from the dancing, and the fresh air was rather appealing after the ballroom's stuffiness. Then she perused the garden, and the temperature was forgotten. "It is snowing!" she exclaimed.

Mr. Darcy squinted into the darkness. "So it is."

Elizabeth hurried to the edge of the terrace, leaning against the balustrade to better view the Marlowes' extensive garden. Naturally, nothing was in bloom at that time of year, but the bare tree branches and ornamental bushes were decorated with a delicate covering of new snow. Torches had been placed at intervals along the garden paths, providing a gentle golden illumination.

"How enchanting!" Elizabeth sighed. "A fresh layer of snow can make anything lovelier. Do you not think so?"

Mr. Darcy regarded her with a most peculiar expression on his face; his lips were slightly parted and his eyes wide. He appeared, for all the world, as if he gazed upon a most wondrous and unusual sight. But he was staring at Elizabeth, not the snow.

"Is the snow not beautiful?" she prompted again.

"Oh yes, yes!" His eyes shifted toward the snow-covered garden below them. "Yes, it is quite pretty."

"Pretty" was a completely inadequate word to describe such a sight, but Elizabeth was not of a mind to quarrel with him. She turned her gaze back to the garden and the snowflakes illuminated in the torches' glow. Fortunately, the terrace was protected from the elements by a roof of sorts, and she was only struck by an occasional wayward snowflake. "I wish I could have a painting of such a scene!" she exclaimed. "It is altogether charming."

"Indeed," he breathed. The wonder on his face would have been more appropriate if he had never before seen such a sight. "Do you know, Miss Bennet, I do not believe I fully appreciated the beauty of snow before this moment."

At least he was finally gazing at the snow. Why was the man so vexing? Most of the time he seemed so distant, but occasionally he would demonstrate how he was not only attending to what Elizabeth said but also taking it to heart. And it was most frustrating. It complicated her propensity to dislike the man and caused her to rethink her opinion of him. As she grew better acquainted with him, the more he puzzled her.

Only when Elizabeth felt a chill did she recall why they were outside: Mr. Darcy had professed a desire to say something to her. What could it be? Customarily there was only one reason a single man would ask to speak privately with a single woman. Her momentary panic was quickly quelled. Mr. Darcy would no more think of marrying Elizabeth than he would consider marrying his cook.

Now she was quite curious about the topic of his desired conversation. And quite cold. "Mr. Darcy, you wished to speak with me about something?" she prompted, wrapping her arms around herself.

He started as if in a reverie and slowly focused his eyes on her. "Yes. Yes, I did. I…" His voice trailed off as his eyes fixed on her…lips? What an odd man.

Still, Elizabeth could not help noticing that he cut a fine figure in his well-tailored coat. And a wayward dark curl over his forehead gave him a completely undeserved rakish appearance. *I could brush it away from his forehead. How would it feel beneath my fingers?* Merciful heavens! How could she entertain such thoughts about Mr. Darcy of all people? Her eyes sought the safer sight of the garden.

"You—" Mr. Darcy cleared his throat and started again. "Your family enjoys some intimacy with Mr. Wickham, I believe."

Elizabeth would not have phrased it so. "I suppose."

"And you…?" Was he asking about the nature of her relationship with Mr. Wickham? The thought made Elizabeth bristle; she did not respond.

His hand, gripping the balustrade, shook noticeably. Why? The other hand ran through his hair, disordering his careful coiffure into a mass of curls. With eyes still fixed on the snow-coated garden, he shook his head sharply as if arguing with himself. "It will not do. I must tell you all," he muttered.

His entire body turned to face her full on. "George Wickham is not a good man," he stated baldly. "His character is deceitful and dissolute. You cannot rely upon anything he tells you."

Elizabeth stiffened and then grew very hot as if her skin itself was boiling. How could Mr. Darcy blacken the man's name further after treating him so horribly? *He* was the reason Mr. Wickham could not join the clergy and was forced into the militia.

It was certainly possible that Mr. Wickham had misrepresented some aspects of the other man's character; after all, every story had two sides. But it could not mitigate the fact that Mr. Darcy had treated the other man abominably with no possible justification.

"He has suffered so much by your hands, and now you undertake to also denigrate his character?" she cried.

"Oh yes, his suffering has been great." Mr. Darcy rolled his eyes and clenched his fists in frustration.

"And at your hands."

Holding himself rigidly, he took a deep breath before speaking slowly and precisely. "I do not know under what circumstances Wickham imposed himself upon you, but I can assure you that his tales were falsehoods."

Now it was Elizabeth's turn to roll her eyes. Mr. Darcy did not know what Mr. Wickham had said. How could he be certain the words were lies?

"I have no desire to engage in idle gossip and speculation. It is unbecoming for a gentleman to be involved in such accusations," he continued. "And there are tales which must remain confidential. But Mr. Wickham is unsuitable company for a lady—or anyone of character. Your family must beware." There was an almost pleading quality to his voice which engendered a pang of guilt in Elizabeth's heart. "You must believe me when I say that Wickham is not to be trusted, and he has brought any misfortune upon himself."

Elizabeth's nascent sympathy for the man evaporated. *Why* must *I believe him? He has done nothing to earn my trust—only belittle me and treat me with disdain. Should I be grateful that he has deigned to dance with me?*

If only she could tell the man what she truly thought of him! But a ball was not an ideal location for a prolonged conflict, and Mr. Darcy was Mr. Bingley's friend. If there were any hope of reuniting Jane with Mr. Bingley, she should not poison his friend's opinion of the Bennet family.

She pressed her lips together, trying to push away her anger. "I thank you for this information and for your concern about my family."

"You will share my words with the rest of your family?" he asked. The hope in his eyes was so evident that she was tempted to believe him—or at least that he believed what he said.

She nodded slowly. "I will tell them what you have said." Although they were no more likely to believe it than Elizabeth was.

Mr. Darcy's entire body relaxed; no doubt he was relieved to be finished with an awkward conversation. "That is all I can ask, thank you." They stared at the garden for a few uncomfortable seconds, then his countenance lightened. "Perhaps you would honor me with another—"

Elizabeth shivered violently. She could not dance with the man again. Although he was an excellent dancer, his company strained her nerves. What excuse could she use to decline his offer?

"Elizabeth!"

They both started at the sound of her Aunt Gardiner's sharp voice. She regarded them with narrowed eyes and arms folded over her chest. "You should come inside. I would not want you to catch a cold." She raked Mr. Darcy with a scathing look, demonstrating that she did not consider him to be an appropriate companion for her niece.

Mr. Darcy stepped away from Elizabeth sheepishly. "Indeed, you should go inside where it is warmer."

"And where there are *more people*," Aunt Gardiner snapped. Did she suspect Mr. Darcy of inappropriate motives? That was one thing

Elizabeth did not have to fear from him. He would do anything to avoid being found in a compromising position with her.

"I beg you to excuse me." With a nod to Elizabeth, Mr. Darcy stalked toward the ballroom.

Aunt Gardiner gave Elizabeth a searching look, but she shrugged, having no desire to repeat Mr. Darcy's words—which amounted to nothing more than an assertion of Mr. Wickham's bad character without any form of proof.

When I return to Longbourn, I will share Mr. Darcy's words with Jane, and we will puzzle out what to share with the family. Mr. Wickham would hardly be a danger to them while he remained in London.

The whole dispute was so strange. Obviously the two men had had some sort of disagreement, but why was Mr. Darcy so intent on blackening Mr. Wickham's name? Was it possible he was jealous? No, that was silly; Mr. Darcy had wealth, power, and the regard of good society. What could possibly spur jealousy?

***

The moment Darcy crossed the threshold into the ballroom, Wickham accosted him and linked arms with him. As if they were two friends idly discussing the latest races or political developments, Wickham walked Darcy about the room. "What are you about?" Wickham murmured in low tones. "Are you whispering poisoned words in Elizabeth's ear?"

"I have nothing to say to you." Darcy tried to discreetly pull his arm from the other man's grip, but Wickham would not release his hold.

Wickham tossed his head. "No matter. She shall not listen to your slanders of my good name. She knows how you malign me."

The confidence in the other man's voice spurred Darcy's doubts. He still did not know what Wickham had told Elizabeth, and she had heard the account from him first. What if she believed him over Darcy?

"I only speak the truth," Darcy said through gritted teeth.

Wickham gave him a rakish smile. "That must be quite galling. To speak the truth and not to be believed."

Darcy fought a desire to strike the other man. Wickham could always provoke him, and he could always read him like a book. Darcy directed his anger toward himself for allowing the other man to notice his attraction to Elizabeth.

Wickham leaned toward Darcy, muttering into his ear. "She will always believe me instead of you, and do you know why?" Darcy said nothing. He did wish to know, but he would not give Wickham the satisfaction. "It is because she is attracted to me. She kissed me, you know…"

Darcy tore himself from Wickham's grasp. "You lie!"

Wickham smirked. "Believe that if you wish. It was in her aunt and uncle's garden…under the oak tree with the split trunk. Her aunt went inside for a moment to speak with the housekeeper…and it would have been more than one kiss if the old woman had not rejoined us so soon."

Darcy's hands twitched with the desire to strike that self-satisfied smile off Wickham's face. He wanted to believe that Wickham lied, that Elizabeth would never permit such liberties. But he could not forget the way she had smiled at him in the Gardiners' drawing room…. And Darcy knew that oak tree; it was visible from the drawing room window. The whole scenario was so sickeningly plausible that Darcy tasted bile.

She never kissed me.

Wickham's smile turned wolfish. "Perhaps I can steal another kiss tonight…with all this mistletoe about…"

Would Elizabeth kiss a man to whom she was not engaged? Or perhaps Wickham had forced a kiss upon her. Cold shivers raced down Darcy's spine, spurring a momentary desire to find Elizabeth and spend every moment protecting her from the other man's advances.

Perhaps it would be simpler and more satisfying to throttle Wickham. If he were unconscious, he could not kiss Elizabeth.

The music had ceased. "Ah, it is time for me to claim my dance with Elizabeth," Wickham said with a smirk.

Darcy considered how he could persuade Wickham to leave Elizabeth alone, but nothing occurred to him. Moving like a predatory animal, Wickham stalked away and was soon lost in the crowd.

Darcy was not accustomed to indecision, but it seemed that every possible reaction to Wickham could only make the situation worse. If he further harangued Elizabeth, she might guess at Darcy's feelings. Without the capacity to act on those feelings, he could not allow her to suspect their existence. And that approach would risk pushing Elizabeth even more firmly into Wickham's arms. Her independence of mind was admirable, but it made her harder to persuade.

As the music commenced, Darcy tortured himself for a minute by watching Elizabeth dance with Wickham. She laughed at something he said, her head tossed back in amusement. Each coy glance Wickham shot her was like a knife to Darcy's stomach.

Wickham was a good dancer, damn him, and Elizabeth, of course, had superlative dancing skills. But Wickham seemed to be crowding her in one direction, breaking them from the line of dancers. How odd.

Oh, he had maneuvered Elizabeth beneath a clump of mistletoe. Wickham reached up to pluck a berry and presented it to Elizabeth. Darcy was too far away to hear what was said, but she gave Wickham a good-natured smile and allowed him to kiss her. It was a quick kiss, a mere brush of the lips before she pulled back. But it was sufficiently long to ignite a fierce ache in Darcy's hollow chest. *Those kisses belong to me! But if I had plucked the berry, would she have been so quick to kiss me?*

Wickham lingered, speaking softly into her ear. Around them the dancers eyed them with tolerant smiles, no doubt believing them to be an engaged couple. Darcy's blood surged hot through his veins, and he locked his knees lest he surrender to the impulse to stride across the intervening distance and rip them apart.

Darcy yearned to stay and claim another dance with Elizabeth, but it would be unwise. His heart was bruised enough with longing for this delightful creature he could not have. If he remained, he was in danger of blurting out his feelings for her—or taking her for a visit to the mistletoe. His kisses would erase every memory of Wickham from her mind.

He tore his gaze from her and fixed his eyes instead on the darkened windows leading to the terrace. He owed his family—and his family name—too much. He could not marry Elizabeth Bennet, and thus it was best not to dance with her. It would only give his foolish heart more encouragement.

At first he had been relieved she had believed his warnings about Wickham so readily, but now he feared that she had not taken them to heart. *I must find another way to convince her without giving rise to expectations. Another day.*

Resolutely, Darcy turned on his heel and stalked toward the exit.

Chapter Four

Four days had passed since the Marlowes' ball, but as she did her needlework Elizabeth still hummed some of the music they had played. She had been blessed by some excellent partners. Mr. Wickham was quite light on his feet and never faltered in the steps. His attentiveness created the illusion that she was the only woman in the room.

Mr. Darcy was an excellent dancer as well, although his attention unsettled her; she did not know why he had sought her out other than to discuss Mr. Wickham, an activity which hardly required dancing. Still, he had been a good partner. In truth, better than Mr. Wickham, although Elizabeth was loath to admit it even to herself. Despite their stilted conversation, they had danced as if made for each other. For a few brief minutes she had felt like she was flying.

No, Elizabeth admonished herself. She could indulge in the memories, but nothing would come of it. Mr. Darcy was attractive, no doubt—with his dark wavy hair and intent dark eyes that somehow always seemed turned in Elizabeth's direction. As they danced, his hands had held her so tenderly, as though she were infinitely precious. But he was too…he was not enough…

When she recalled dancing with Mr. Darcy, she found it difficult to remember her objections to him. No. Elizabeth shook her head. She should not be silly about this. An attractive man danced well; there was nothing more to say.

She turned her thoughts to the more promising subject of Mr. Wickham. In the carriage on the way home from the ball, Aunt Gardiner had observed, "I believe you have made a conquest there."

Elizabeth was not so certain; he had neglected to dance with her when he had promised—although he had explained that faux pas by saying the pretty blonde woman had been spurned by another man; Mr. Wickham had partnered her to lift her spirits. Certainly, he possessed an easy air and a delightful countenance; his attentions to Elizabeth seemed sincere. Yet she felt little attachment to him. She waited to be overwhelmed with her feelings as Jane was with Mr. Bingley, but nothing had happened.

Now I am being fanciful again. My expectations are too high; not everyone in the world is destined for such love. Mr. Wickham was pleasant company—far pleasanter than Mr. Darcy. Most likely nothing would come of it. Elizabeth would enjoy the soldier's company and return to Hertfordshire with naught to show but memories of a few flirtations.

When her Uncle Gardiner strolled into the drawing room, both Elizabeth and her aunt looked up from their needlework. He sat heavily in an armchair before speaking. "Well, Madeline, I told you I wrote to my brother Bennet." He waved a letter.

Elizabeth sat up straighter. Why had Uncle Gardiner corresponded with her father?

Her uncle fixed his gaze on Elizabeth. "This concerns you as well, Lizzy. At the Marlowes' ball, your aunt was most concerned about the animosity between Mr. Wickham and Mr. Darcy—and how they both wished to involve you in their dispute."

Elizabeth stabbed her needle into the cloth rather more forcefully than required. Mr. Darcy had already intruded sufficiently into her life, and she had no desire to discuss him with her aunt and uncle.

Her uncle continued, "I wrote to your father to obtain his opinion on the matter." Adjusting his spectacles, he read from the letter. "'I have not heard one word uttered against Mr. Wickham in Hertfordshire. All who know him consider him to be a pleasant and well-mannered man who has been mistreated by the Darcy family. Mr. Darcy, however, is a proud, unpleasant man who was generally disliked in Hertfordshire society. I have no reason or inclination to believe his word over that of Mr. Wickham.'"

Elizabeth gave a slow nod. "I am inclined to believe Mr. Wickham as well. The two men have quarreled in the past about matters that are of importance to Mr. Darcy, but I cannot imagine they are as dire as he portrays. Nor am I inclined to discontinue my association with Mr. Wickham."

"I am glad to hear you say that. I would be most sorry to banish Mr. Wickham from my house." Uncle Gardiner's eyes twinkled.

Aunt Gardiner frowned. "I have never heard that Mr. Darcy is untrustworthy; however, I do not like his attentions to you, Lizzy. It is hard to conceive that his intentions are honorable."

Elizabeth felt a frisson of anxiety. She was inclined to believe that he sought her company primarily to sneer at her country manners and lack of polish, but perhaps he did possess deeper, darker motives which would be served by warning her about Mr. Wickham.

Mr. Darcy did not appear to be the type to seduce women for the pleasure of it, but many of his class were. What did Elizabeth know of it?

Her uncle stood but handed a letter to Elizabeth before quitting the room. "Here is a note from your mother, which was enclosed along with my letter. I shall leave you to it."

Dropping her needlework in her lap, Elizabeth slowly opened the letter and read its contents.

My dear Lizzy,

All are well at Longbourn, although the house is much quieter with you away. Lydia and Kitty are making some good friends among the militia. Unfortunately, Mr. Wickham is away on a fortnight's leave. Your sisters are such favorites with the officers. They understand that your father will not live forever and that they must secure suitable husbands when they can.

Charlotte Lucas—now Charlotte Collins—was married in a small ceremony on Sunday. Her father spared no expense on wedding clothes or flowers, and it was enough to make her look almost less plain. They are gone into Kent, where Mr. Collins apparently has a very nice parsonage. And, of course, Mrs. Collins may look forward to the day when she is mistress of Longbourn. It pains me to think—let alone write— such a thing, particularly when one of my own daughters might have claimed that position. Lady Lucas will not stop crowing her triumph over having one daughter married whereas I have none.

I hope you are employing your time in London to great advantage and meeting suitable young men. Otherwise you might as well have stayed at home and we should have sent Lydia.

Yours, etc.
Mama

Elizabeth crumpled the paper into a ball, ignoring her aunt's surprised stare. Her mother never lost an opportunity to chastise her second-oldest daughter for refusing Mr. Collins. Although Elizabeth knew it had been the right decision, regret and guilt weighed upon her.

Such constant remonstrances had been one of the reasons Elizabeth had sought refuge in London, but distance did not completely alleviate the guilt gnawing in her stomach. Her mother was not wrong that Elizabeth's marriage to Mr. Collins would have provided her family with the security that they now lacked.

If Papa should pass away while all five of us were unmarried, it would be a terrible tangle. I cannot not imagine how we would all manage. Unbidden, all sorts of visions arose in Elizabeth's mind: becoming a governess, marrying a shopkeeper, living as a dependent relative—even the poor house. At the time of Mr. Collins's proposal, Elizabeth had believed that Mr. Bingley was sincerely attached to Jane and would make her an offer—and he certainly could care for the Bennet women should the worst occur. Now that eventuality seemed highly unlikely.

Unequal to the task of discussing the letter with her aunt, Elizabeth picked up her needlework once more but could not see clearly enough to resume the task. The brightly colored threads blurred and swam in her vision. Her mother should not blame her for the family's situation, but that did not prevent Elizabeth's niggling doubts.

If her father perished, Mr. Collins would inherit. Even with Charlotte as a moderating influence, very little could stop him from descending upon the Bennet family like a vulture onto a carcass. Elizabeth shuddered. She could not recall Mr. Collins's sweaty hands and greasy hair without disgust, yet surely she could endure far worse to ensure her family's safety. Now they had nothing.

Well, perhaps not nothing. Mr. Wickham's interest might be sincere. Of course, his pay was a pittance, but at least he would take responsibility and help support her family. As his wife, at the very least Elizabeth would not be a burden to her mother—or any other family members who might feel obligated to care for them. With a husband to provide for her, Elizabeth would be independent and in a position to help the others.

Her eyes lit on the bare branches of the large oak tree outside the window and the rose bushes beyond. Occasionally she felt uneasy about Mr. Wickham's character, but his treatment at Mr. Darcy's hands was reason enough for bitterness. The militia officer had open, pleasing manners and was amiable and easy to converse with. Elizabeth did not love him, but she was reasonably certain she could be content as his wife. Then she could be a help rather than a hindrance to her family.

She pressed her lips together in a thin line. Yes, it was decided. If Mr. Wickham made her an offer, she would accept.

***

Darcy crumpled the note in his fist. He had engaged a man to follow Wickham about London, and the man's notes reported that in the five days since the Marlowes' ball, Wickham had been twice received at the Gardiners' house. Damnation! His words to Elizabeth had not been taken seriously. Darcy had intended to visit her immediately after the ball, but an emergency with flooding at Pemberley had required him to ride to Derbyshire. He had only returned a few hours earlier.

There was a knock at the door before Ward, the footman, entered, his manner as stiff as the servant's livery he wore. "Mr. Wickham is here to see you."

Words guaranteed to ruin Darcy's day. The sheer gall of that man astounded him.

"He called several times while you were away, sir. Should I tell him you are still not at home?" Ward asked.

It was tempting, but a conversation with Wickham might yield some clues about what the man planned. "No. I will see him, but he will not be staying long." Darcy stood. "Where is Miss Darcy?" Georgiana should not encounter Wickham at Darcy House.

"She is visiting friends with Mrs. Annesley."

Thank God. "Station someone outside the front door to intercept them should they arrive while he is here." Ward nodded. "Where did you put Wickham?"

"I considered the stables, sir, but ended up with the blue drawing room."

Darcy smiled at his footman's joke. "I knew there was a reason I kept you on."

"Yes, sir." Ward's face was impassive, but his lips twitched with humor.

Darcy reached for the coat he had discarded on a chair and shrugged it on. Managing Wickham required Darcy to be every inch the master of Pemberley.

Ward followed Darcy as he thumped down the grand front stairs into the marble-clad front hall. Darcy stalked grimly toward the blue drawing room door, squaring his shoulders and throwing open the door.

Wickham lounged insouciantly on a fainting sofa, looking for all the world like the picture of gentlemanly idleness. "Ah…Darcy," he drawled, "so good of you to see me."

He does not even stand to greet the master of the house, his host! Darcy gritted his teeth. He could not allow Wickham's petty insults to irk him. "What do you want, Wickham?"

Wickham gestured grandly to the opposite settee—*Darcy's* settee. "Have a seat and we can talk over old times."

I will not allow him to provoke me. Darcy took a deep breath as if he could inhale patience. "You have one minute to tell me what you want before I throw you out of Darcy House."

Wickham huffed. "No chewing over fond old memories?" He clutched his heart theatrically. "You wound me!"

"Wickham," Darcy growled as he advanced menacingly toward the man.

"Very well." Wickham sat upright on the sofa, holding up his hands in a gesture of surrender. "I came to make you an offer."

"I am not interested."

"You have not heard the offer."

"I am not interest—"

"Even if it concerns Elizabeth Bennet?"

Damn the man! Just the sound of her name made Darcy's heart beat faster. "You could not possibly have any interest in Elizabeth Bennet," Darcy scoffed, trying to keep his voice from shaking.

Wickham gave him a sly smile. "But I do, I assure you. I have a business proposition which concerns her deeply."

Darcy walked away from Wickham—away from the temptation to strike him—positioning himself so a chair stood between them. He grasped the back of the chair so tightly that his fingers turned white. "A business proposition?"

"Indeed." Wickham stood. They were almost of a height, putting him at Darcy's eye level. "I will agree not to make Elizabeth Bennet an offer of marriage if you will pay off my gambling debts."

"You bastard." It was amazing how quickly anger could turn to fear. Darcy's breath came in ragged gasps, and his hands were slick with perspiration against the wood of the chair. "Elizabeth would not accept a marriage proposal from you." He intended to toss the words out with force and scorn, but with such uneven breath behind them, they sounded weak and strangled.

Wickham laughed. "Shall I test that assertion?"

Darcy's trembling fingers clutched the chair more forcefully. Wickham had visited the Gardiners' house twice in five days. He had danced with Elizabeth at the Marlowes' ball and kissed her there. He had kissed her under the oak tree…

Have I already lost Elizabeth? My Elizabeth?

Darcy teetered on the edge of a precipice, in danger of falling into complete despair.

"I kissed her…and more…" Wickham's voice drawled suggestively. "Yesterday, in the Gardiners' drawing room when we were alone for a few minutes. She smiled at me…such a sweet smile…"

As the other man spoke, Darcy could envision it all too easily: Wickham's head bent over Elizabeth's, his hand under her chin. Her head raised to receive his kiss…

"Stop!" Darcy cried, provoking a knowing smirk from Wickham. "You should not speak so disrespectfully about a well-bred lady."

Wickham spread his arms wide. "It is but the truth."

"And you are a proficient liar."

"I do not lie about everything."

With no easy response to this, Darcy stared at the floor, silent for a long minute. Hopefully his breaths were not as loud to Wickham as they seemed to him. "How much?" Darcy finally asked in a voice that seemed scraped over rocks.

"Fifteen thousand."

"Fifteen thousand!" Darcy's head jerked up. Wickham grinned lazily. "You could not possibly have accumulated so much in debts."

The other man shrugged. "I gamble frequently." No doubt Wickham intended to realize a tidy profit from this scheme.

I could do it, but it would hurt. It would mean delaying plans for improvements to the western cottages at Pemberley, halting construction of the new bridge, canceling the gift of Georgiana's pianoforte…

Wickham was still smirking at him, pleased to have him at a disadvantage. The officer had no plans to make Elizabeth an offer, Darcy realized. He wanted to extort money to prevent an action he never planned to take. A pretty scheme indeed.

Darcy released his death grip on the chair, standing straighter. "I will not pay you a shilling. You have no intention of marrying Elizabeth Bennet."

"Is that what you believe?" Wickham raised an eyebrow.

"She has no dowry to speak of, nothing to tempt you."

Wickham did not flinch. Instead, his hand idly traced the ruffle at his cuff. "Perhaps her charms alone are enough to tempt me."

"You want nothing other than money," Darcy said firmly.

"Are you so certain of that?"

"Do not importune me again. This matter is closed." Darcy stalked to the door and opened it, an unsubtle hint.

"Very well." With a sigh, Wickham retrieved his hat and greatcoat from a nearby chair. "If that is what you choose to believe…" He sauntered toward Darcy until they were only a foot apart. "I shall make certain you receive an invitation to the wedding—"

Darcy had not planned to punch Wickham. It was as if his arm acted of its own accord. But the words, the smug expression, and the air of triumph combined to snap the reins on Darcy's temper.

Darcy's fist hit Wickham's chin with a satisfying, meaty thump, and the other man slid to the floor with a cry. Ward and another footman burst into the room, but when they saw Wickham on the floor, they stayed near the doorway, gaping.

Wickham slowly climbed to his feet, cradling his chin in one hand. "I hope you found that punch satisfying, Darcy, because you just ensured that"—he eyed the footmen warily—"the thing you do not wish to happen will happen. Immediately."

Before Darcy could reply, Wickham pushed himself between the two footmen and into the front hall. His footsteps thumped loudly on the marble floor until the front door opened and closed.

"Should we stop him, sir?" Ward inquired.

"No, the last thing I need is more Wickham in my house," Darcy responded, cradling his right hand. Wickham had a tough jaw.

Darcy dismissed the footmen and concentrated his attention on slowing his rapid breathing and fluttering heartbeat. Striking Wickham had been wrong. It might drive Wickham to make Elizabeth an offer in a fit of pique—even if he had no intention of following through on a wedding. But he would not marry her. Wickham wanted a rich wife more than he wanted revenge on Darcy. Did he not?

Darcy hated that he could not be sure of the answer.

The drawing room door burst open, and an agitated Georgiana rushed in. "Was that Mr. Wickham leaving Darcy House?"

Darcy nodded wearily. "Yes."

"Granger would not allow us to enter Darcy House, and then Wickham rushed out in high dudgeon!" Georgiana's face was flushed with agitation. "He was so upset he did not even stop to leer at me."

Darcy laughed at his sister's joke. "I am sorry you had to see him." Darcy enclosed his sister in an embrace. "I wanted to be rid of him before you arrived home."

Georgiana made a disparaging noise. "I am not a china doll, William. I do not fear him; he can do nothing to me now."

Darcy released her and walked to the sideboard where they kept a decanter of brandy. "I am glad to hear you say that, dear heart." He poured the liquid into a crystal glass and took a bracing swallow.

"But why was he here?" Darcy did not reply immediately; there was no need to worry her about business that did not concern her. "Was it about me?" she asked in a small voice.

"No, of course not."

Her forehead wrinkled. "It *was* about me! You are simply trying to protect me again."

"No, no." Darcy rubbed his forehead.

"Tell me what his business was, or I cannot believe your denials." Georgiana crossed her arms.

Darcy sighed. Why not? He had nobody else to confide in. "Very well." He sank into an armchair and gestured for her to do the same. Once they were seated, it took him a moment to order his thoughts. "George Wickham came to me with a proposition. He wanted me to pay him so that he would not propose to a certain young lady. Miss Elizabeth Bennet."

"Not propose to…?" Georgiana's brows knit together. "Why in the world would you pay for that?"

Darcy bit his lip. "Wickham suspects…I have an interest in the woman's well-being."

Georgiana appeared even more confused. "What sort of interest?"

Darcy studied his glass. "Er…romantic."

"Oh!" Georgiana's hand flew to her mouth. "Oh." After a moment she swallowed. "And do you? Have a romantic interest in her?"

Now he stared at the fire. This conversation was mortifying enough without having to meet Georgiana's eyes. "I do…admire her. But her family is…undesirable. I cannot possibly…" His voice trailed off, but then he cleared his throat. "I cannot make her an offer."

"Oh." Georgiana contemplated this. "Is she a maidservant?"

"What?" Darcy exclaimed. "No! Of course not."

"A shopgirl or a governess?"

What did his sister think of him? "No. Her father is a gentleman."

"Then I do not see why it is a problem." Georgiana folded her hands in her lap.

"Her father has little property to speak of and only daughters, so his fortune is entailed away from his family line. And her mother's family is from trade."

Georgiana regarded him thoughtfully, her head tilted to one side. "Mr. Bingley's family is from trade."

Darcy waved irritably. "But it was longer ago, and the Bingleys are wealthier. And the Bennets' behavior is sometimes…inappropriate."

"But surely Elizabeth's is not."

"No. Not at all."

Georgiana shrugged. "You would not be proposing to her family."

Darcy pinched the bridge of his nose. "It is complicated. There are many good reasons I cannot make her an offer."

"If you say so." She sat silent for a moment. "And Mr. Wickham is threatening to propose to her?"

Darcy nodded. "He suspects my interest in her and sees this as an opportunity to thwart me. He was quite angry when I refused to pay him…also after I punched him."

"You punched him?" Georgiana clapped her hands gleefully. "Good for you! I wish I could punch him."

"Perhaps there will be a future opportunity," Darcy remarked dryly.

"But certainly Miss Bennet will not accept him!" Georgiana exclaimed, her eyes round with horror.

Darcy's lack of certainty must have shown on his face.

"But you must have warned her!"

"I did." Darcy took a big gulp of brandy. "But Wickham is still welcome at her uncle's house. I fear she did not take my warning seriously."

"You did not tell her about me," Georgiana said in a small voice.

"Of course not!"

Georgiana stood and walked to the window, gazing down on the street. Darcy watched her every move; Wickham's appearance was bound to stir up bad memories. Finally, she cleared her throat. "You should."

That was the last thing Darcy expected to hear. "Dearest? Are you certain?" Georgiana had always been adamant about complete secrecy.

She rested her forehead against the glass. "Yes," she said in a tremulous voice. "If my story might save other women from Wickham, it should be shared."

Darcy quickly considered the ramifications. If he could be open with Elizabeth about how Wickham had taken advantage of Georgiana, then she would understand why she needed to shun Wickham. Darcy launched himself from his chair, crossed the room, and gave his sister a kiss on the cheek. "Thank you, dearest. You do not know what this means to me."

She smiled. "It is the least I can do for the woman you love."

Darcy froze before releasing his grip on his sister's shoulders. "What say you?"

"It is the least I can do for the woman you love," she repeated in a more quizzical tone.

His mouth opened, a denial on the tip of his tongue. *Yes, I like her. Yes, I greatly admire her. But...*

The words would not come.

As he considered the past few months, he realized that Georgiana had identified the odd sensation he had been unable to name. The rush of excitement when he anticipated being in her presence. The peace that settled over him when they were in company. The disappointment when they must part. The thrill that shot through his body at the sound of her voice or the glimpse of her face.

"I love her..." he said in wonder, each word right and true.

"Of course, you do," Georgiana retorted. "I thought you knew that."

"You are wise beyond your years," Darcy said and dropped a kiss on the top of her head.

He left the room at a brisk pace; there was no time to waste.

Chapter Five

"Mr. Wickham is here, ma'am."

Aunt Gardiner nodded to the maid to escort their visitor into the drawing room. Elizabeth's stomach fluttered with excitement. This would be her first opportunity to see the handsome officer since resolving that she would accept his proposal—if he made one.

"Ladies." Mr. Wickham gave a courtly bow upon entering the room. He was wearing his regimentals. Elizabeth had laughed when Lydia and Kitty sighed over officers in red coats, but they did flatter the male figure and render the wearer more distinguished. And, of course, Mr. Wickham's features were very regular, and his entire air was so pleasing.

Still, he was not quite as handsome as Mr. Darcy. He lacked...*something* she saw in the other man's eyes when he looked upon her, although she knew not what to call it. There was no doubt of the prodigious intelligence behind Mr. Darcy's dark eyes; he constantly observed and evaluated everything around him, much as Elizabeth did herself. And when he turned that knowing gaze on her...

A little flushed, Elizabeth inched her chair away from the fireplace.

"Miss Bennet?" Mr. Wickham was trying to catch her attention. How long had she been staring into space?

How stupid to think of Mr. Darcy when he was not here and was unlikely to ever be here. He was indeed handsome and intelligent, but it was irrelevant. Mr. Wickham was here, and Mr. Darcy was not.

Focusing her attention on their visitor, she noticed a red mark on his chin. "Are you all right, Mr. Wickham?" she inquired, pointing to her own chin.

The man touched the red spot gingerly. "Just a trifle. I fell this morning and hit my chin on a table in the barracks. I am fortunate it was not worse."

Aunt Gardiner rang for tea. The conversation was convivial and interesting—everything that good company should be. Mr. Wickham's bon mots wrung laughter from Elizabeth and her aunt more than once. He inquired after her aunt's oldest child, who had been sick with a cold, and asked Elizabeth of news from Longbourn.

When the teacups were empty, and the biscuits were reduced to crumbs, Elizabeth became aware of a peculiar intensity in the man's eyes.

"It is an especially mild day for December," he addressed Elizabeth with a grin. "Would you accompany me for a walk about the Gardiners' fine garden? I have often noticed parts of that handsome oak tree from the window, but I never had an opportunity to see the whole thing."

Elizabeth glanced at her aunt, not at all sure it would be proper to be alone with Mr. Wickham, but Aunt Gardiner smiled benevolently. "Indeed, it is too nice a day to pass it all indoors. Go and enjoy the garden. I shall check on Harry."

Soon Elizabeth found herself behind the Gardiners' house with only a light shawl around her shoulders; however, the bright sunshine warmed her and the air around her. The snow that had fallen the night of the ball had melted long ago, and the only clouds were white and fluffy. Mr. Wickham offered Elizabeth his arm, and they strolled along a meandering path through the garden.

The house's garden was much larger than was usual for the neighborhood. Both Mr. and Mrs. Gardiner had spent their childhoods in the countryside, and they had purchased a house with an unusually large parcel of land.

It was beautifully maintained. Mrs. Gardiner did much of the work herself with some help from their manservant. Of course, many of the plants were dormant for the winter, but there was a pleasant walk lined with shrubberies, vibrantly green against the dull brown of the winter grass, and several holly trees with variegated leaves. A large, double-trunked oak tree dominated the center of the garden, spreading its limbs majestically over everything below it.

"This is lovely," Mr. Wickham said after they had wandered for a minute.

"Yes. I miss Hertfordshire when I am in London, but the garden is my consolation."

"Do you believe you would always wish to live near Longbourn?"

Elizabeth's heart sped up. *Why is he suddenly curious about my future?* "I enjoy traveling and seeing different parts of the country. I suppose I could settle anywhere given the right inducement."

"And what would be the right inducement?" His voice was low, making the words sound almost seductive.

Why was her mouth so dry? "Well, of course, if I were to marry someone from another part of the country."

Mr. Wickham stopped walking, gently pulling on her gloved hand so she would face him. The unexpected contact made her blush.

"What if you were to marry a soldier who had no fixed home but moved from place to place?"

"A s-soldier?" Elizabeth echoed. "I d-do not suppose you mean Mr. Denny."

He laughed gently. "Your wit is one of many things I love about you."

Her breath caught.

Mr. Wickham smiled. "Yes, I use that word deliberately. I cannot possibly express how greatly I love and esteem you. And you would make me the happiest man on earth if you would consent to be my wife."

Elizabeth had imagined this moment. She had believed herself prepared for the possibility. But she realized in a rush that she was not ready; it would have been far better if he had not asked the question. It had been easier to decide the question hypothetically than to be faced with the actuality.

She did not love Mr. Wickham, but she admired him. Perhaps she could love him in time. She had vowed to marry for love, but such a vow would not help her family if they were left penniless and alone. She could do far worse than a charming and attentive husband like Mr. Wickham. He was not wealthy, of course, but he was sure to do well enough. Elizabeth had never fostered any grand hopes of marrying an earl's son or a viscount. And she could not imagine informing her mother that she had declined yet another eligible offer of marriage.

She gazed into his warm brown eyes, so caring and full of love for her. Mr. Collins's words echoed in her ears: "It is by no means certain that another offer of marriage may ever be made to you." In the privacy of her mind, she had acknowledged the truth in his words; but now, miraculously, she *had* received another proposal. It would be foolish to think a third offer would come her way. Mr. Darcy would certainly never propose.

Mr. Darcy? Why am I thinking of him at this moment? But she could not completely suppress the pang of something—regret, perhaps—when she thought of him. *No, he looks at me only to criticize. He does not even like me. He is irrelevant.*

Noticing Mr. Wickham's stricken countenance, Elizabeth realized she had long been silent. "Do you perhaps require some time to think about it?" he asked hesitantly.

"No."

Now he looked even more stricken.

She took a deep breath. "No—I mean…I do not require more time. My answer is yes."

***

Far too impatient to wait while his own carriage was made ready, Darcy took a cab to Gracechurch Street. During the ride he considered how to introduce such a delicate subject to a well-bred lady—likely two well-bred ladies since Mrs. Gardiner would almost certainly insist on being a chaperone.

Darcy was confident his plan was good, but doubt gnawed in the back of his mind. What if Wickham had immediately left Darcy House to propose to Elizabeth? Darcy's mind shied away from the very thought, but he forced himself to consider the possibility. What if Elizabeth had accepted Wickham's offer? The mere thought plunged Darcy into icy water.

Elizabeth would not break such a promise lightly; she would not end an engagement simply upon Darcy's word. Darcy could not help spinning out a future for Elizabeth as Wickham's betrothed. Wickham was unlikely to follow through on a promise of marriage, which would cause a scandal. It was the way of the world to blame the woman in such circumstances, and many women never recovered their social standing after a broken engagement. Elizabeth might lose all opportunities to make a respectable match after that. Most likely her parents would ship her away to live with some distant relative or find an obliging clerk in her Uncle Gardiner's business to marry her quickly and quietly. She deserved so much more….

And if Wickham *did* marry her…such a future was not worth contemplating.

Darcy's chest felt tight as his heart ached for this imaginary future Elizabeth. *I must prevent it. I must.*

He stared out of the window; why could the cab not go any faster? The carriage rattled and stuttered over cobblestones. What could he do if she had already accepted Wickham? Darcy dropped his head in his hands, trying to ward off a sense of dread. Perhaps there would be nothing he could do in such a situation.

Darcy clutched the door handle as the carriage lurched around a sharp corner. What if she loved Wickham? Darcy's stomach churned sickeningly, and he closed his eyes, praying fervently that such was not the case.

The carriage swayed up to the front of the Gardiners' house, and Darcy leapt from it the moment it stopped. He handed the driver some coins and was striding to the door before the carriage even rattled away.

The maid who answered the door looked at him wide-eyed.

"Mr. Darcy to see Miss Elizabeth Bennet."

The maid curtsied and admitted him to the front hallway as she scurried away to find her mistress. Darcy shifted his weight, barely noticing anything in the elegant but narrow room. Although he was unsure where this sense of urgency sprang from, he wanted to see Elizabeth immediately and ensure she was safe from Wickham.

"Mrs. Gardiner will see you in the drawing room," the maid said and beckoned for him to follow her down the hallway. *Mrs. Gardiner but not Miss Bennet? Is Elizabeth ill? Has she been summoned home for a family emergency? Is she refusing to see me?*

The older woman was standing and facing the door when Darcy entered the room. "Mr. Darcy," she said with a tight smile, "to what do we owe this honor?"

Darcy was too impatient for common social niceties. "I must see Elizabeth—Miss Elizabeth—immediately."

Mrs. Gardiner's eyebrow rose. She was definitely suspicious of Darcy's intentions. "She is not available now. Perhaps you could return tomorrow."

Not available? That was not the same thing as not at home. "Thank you, no. The matter is most urgent. I will remain until she is available." He eyed the sofa as if preparing for a long wait.

Mrs. Gardiner pursed her mouth, evidently displeased at the prospect of Darcy occupying her drawing room for hours on end. "Mr. Darcy—" she began in a quelling tone.

A flash of something caught Darcy's attention from the corner of his eye, and he shot a glance toward the window. There had been movement. Elizabeth's white dress stood out vividly against the browns and greens of the garden, but she was not alone.

It was a scene from Darcy's worst nightmare. Wickham was talking to her earnestly, and she was smiling at him. But that was not the worst.

The worst was that he was holding her hand.

And she was smiling.

Darcy was racing for the door before he had consciously decided to do so. *I must get to Elizabeth. Now.*

"Mr. Darcy! Where are you going?" Mrs. Gardiner followed him out of the room.

Naturally, Darcy was unfamiliar with the house, but he guessed there would be a back door to the garden. He rushed along the only corridor that led to the back of the house and...yes, there was a back door.

"Mr. Darcy!" The maid had joined her mistress, and they both called his name as they gave chase. But panic had given him wings, and they were far too slow to catch him.

He twisted the door handle violently, and it opened, spilling him into the garden. Once outside, he ran, dodging shrubs and randomly placed rocks, desperate to reach the back of the garden where he had espied Elizabeth and Wickham.

"Beckett! Beckett! We need your help!" Mrs. Gardiner cried. No doubt Beckett was some sort of manservant. *Do they think that one man can stop me from reaching Elizabeth? Ha, I would like to see Beckett try.*

As he rounded a curve in the pathway, his quarry came into view. They were already staring in his direction, no doubt alerted by the shouting.

"Mr. Darcy?" Elizabeth's mouth fell open.

However, Wickham was grinning smugly. "You are too late, Darcy. She is mine now."

Chapter Six

Elizabeth did not know what to think. One minute she and Mr. Wickham—George—were having a simple conversation about when to hold the marriage ceremony as Elizabeth sought to quell the anxious fluttering in her stomach. A minute later they heard shouting, and Mr. Darcy came pelting in their direction from the house.

"You are too late, Darcy. She is mine now," George said.

What did that mean? Elizabeth was not George's possession like a table or a horse. And why would Mr. Darcy care?

Mr. Darcy stumbled to a stop, staring at them. No, at their joined hands. Elizabeth lifted her chin slightly, refusing to let go. Engaged couples could hold hands; it was not improper.

"He made you an offer?" Mr. Darcy asked her. She nodded, not feeling equal to a verbal response. "And you accepted?" She nodded again. As they spoke, her Aunt Gardiner hurried up behind Mr. Darcy, swiftly followed by Shaw, the housemaid, and Beckett, the manservant. Had they been attempting to prevent Mr. Darcy from entering the garden? Why was he here? Hoping for elucidation, Elizabeth peered at Mr. Darcy and instantly wished she had not.

His face held an expression of the bleakest despair. As if he had lost something of great value and knew he would never retrieve it. His devastation was so complete that Elizabeth dropped George's hand and took an involuntary step forward to comfort him. George caught her arm and murmured "Elizabeth" sternly. Oh yes, an engaged woman should not comfort another man.

Mr. Darcy's chest was heaving, and he glared at George as if he could incinerate the other man with his gaze. "Go ahead, hit me again," George said with a smile, tapping the red mark on his chin. *Was that how he had obtained it? Had he not said...?* "You will still be too late."

However, Mr. Darcy did not look like a man about to punch his nemesis. He looked like a man who was about to jump off a bridge into the Thames, but for the life of her, Elizabeth could not understand why. Why should her engagement to George prompt such despair?

Mr. Darcy closed his eyes, rubbing his face with shaking hands. Then he released a long breath, his shoulders relaxing. A sort of half-smile curved his lips. "If there is a scandal, so be it," he murmured to himself. *What did he mean by that?*

When he opened his eyes again, they were fixed on Elizabeth, a darker color than she had ever seen before. It was as if she were in a cage with a tiger—a tiger who had selected her as his prey and would ignore everything else until he caught her. The skin on the back of her neck prickled with unease.

Mr. Darcy's expression must have unsettled George as well. "Darcy," he said in a warning tone, but the other man gave no indication he heard. They were a still tableau for a few seconds.

When Mr. Darcy moved, it was sudden and swift. Before Elizabeth could blink, he was standing in front of her. In another heartbeat, his arms were wrapped around her. Over the rush of blood pounding in her ears, Elizabeth could hear Aunt Gardiner and George shouting, but she could only stare, mesmerized, into Mr. Darcy's eyes.

"Forgive me, Elizabeth," he whispered, his hot breath tickling her ear.

"Forgive you for wh—?" Mr. Darcy's mouth was upon hers before she could finish the sentence. Elizabeth had been kissed before, but comparing those paltry offerings to this overwhelming experience would be like comparing a tiny rivulet to the Thames.

Despite a faint voice at the back of her head warning that this was wrong, she was flooded with a sense of rightness. This was the way kissing should be. She should kiss this man forever and never stop.

But then her body demanded more…more touching…more contact. Touching with lips and tongues was not nearly sufficient. They were too far apart. Her body pressed into his, her softness against the hard planes of his chest and the muscles of his legs. Her hand traveled up his back to tangle in his hair, which was every bit as soft as she had imagined.

But these touches were still not sufficient. Her body—her core—tingled and grew warm as if demanding a different kind of contact with the extremely male body opposite hers. Kissing was not enough. Touching through clothing was not enough. She needed to touch his skin—without the barrier of clothing—and have him touch her, exploring each other's bodies until they merged together into one.

Oh, merciful heavens! What am I thinking? Where are these blatantly carnal thoughts arising from? Did kissing always have this effect? But no, the stolen kiss with John Lucas had not been like this. And kissing Mr. Wickham…

Mr. Wickham.

George!

Her fiancé!

Oh, goodness, I am kissing Mr. Darcy in front of my new fiancé. Enthusiastically.

Even with that panicked thought in her head, it took a moment for her body to obey her command and pull away from the kiss. Even then she did not struggle in Mr. Darcy's firm embrace. He touched his forehead to hers as their hearts pounded and their breaths came in ragged gasps.

Mr. Darcy straightened, glancing at her and glaring at George. "It is not enough," he muttered to himself. "I must do more. I must make certain. Forgive me, Elizabeth."

This was all the warning she had before his mouth plundered hers again. His taste and scent filled her senses, and she could do nothing but enjoy the sensations.

And then she felt his hands. On her waist! Scandalous. He was caressing her through the thin fabric of her dress—in front of at least four witnesses.

She ripped herself from his grasp. "Mr. Darcy!" she cried, outraged.

Backing away, his hands in the air, Mr. Darcy could not have appeared more contrite. "I apologize. It was the only way to be sure..."

Elizabeth did not know what he was talking about, but she was well aware of her feelings about his actions. She curved her fingers into a fist—and punched him in the mouth.

***

Darcy had been prepared for a slap, but the punch was a surprise.

He stumbled backward with the force of the blow, pressing his fingers to his lower lip. They came away bloody. But no matter; he would endure far more for Elizabeth's sake.

She stared at him, horrified, her chest heaving and her face flushed with anger. Then she very deliberately wiped her lips with the back of her hand, removing all trace of his kisses. She was magnificent. Many other women would have collapsed in a gibbering heap of nerves, but not his Elizabeth.

And she was *his* Elizabeth now. He had ensured it. In that instant after the horrible discovery that he had arrived too late to prevent the engagement, Darcy had realized he would far rather marry her and risk the disgrace of an alliance with the Bennets than see her wed to Wickham.

Pulling out a handkerchief, Darcy applied it to the cut on his lip. Only then did he turn to gauge the reactions of their witnesses. At some point Mr. Gardiner had joined the group. Darcy could picture a kitchen boy being sent running to fetch the man from his warehouse.

Gardiner regarded Darcy with an outraged expression, his hands folded over his chest. Mrs. Gardiner seemed close to tears—causing Darcy a moment of regret—her hand over her mouth. The maid seemed to think this was the most entertaining thing she had seen in years, and perhaps it was. The manservant's forehead was creased with anxiety; perhaps he was concerned that someone would order him to lay hands on Darcy.

And Wickham…his expression was beyond description. If Darcy were not so anxious about Elizabeth's reaction, he would have reveled in Wickham's. The man was drawing deep, measured breaths through his nose and glaring daggers at Darcy. He knew he had been bested. Darcy would be quite pleased…

If it were not for the hateful glare from the woman he loved.

Elizabeth had her hands crossed over her chest as if to protect it from further inappropriate advances on his part. Tears glistened in her eyes, but she did not weep. In fact, she appeared liable to punch him again. He would let her. He deserved it.

And he would do it all again in a heartbeat.

Mr. Gardiner stepped forward, attempting to take charge of the situation. "Mr. Darcy!" he thundered, his body shaking in indignation. "How dare you treat my niece in such an infamous fashion? I-I ought to have you arrested!"

No doubt if Darcy were someone else, Gardiner would have him arrested; rank did have its privileges.

Darcy felt the heat rising in his face. It was difficult to defend himself when he knew his behavior was wrong, but he had done what was necessary to save Elizabeth. "I apologize to you, Mr. Gardiner, and to you, Miss Bennet." Elizabeth's eyes were averted from him. "I-I did not arrive with the purpose of engaging in such indecent behavior. But I…"

His words trickled to a halt. How could he possibly explain it? The truth—"I was saving your niece from Mr. Wickham"—would be both difficult to explain and readily denied by the man himself. "I did what was necessary," he finished finally.

"Necessary?" Gardiner spat out. "You have compromised my niece! What necessity could possibly provoke such actions? You may be accustomed to enjoying such licentious behavior with impunity, but I assure you, sir, that it is not acceptable in my house!"

Darcy's shoulders stiffened, and he reminded himself that the man had every right to his indignation. But he did loathe the assumption that he was a rake of the first order. "I am prepared to do my duty to Eliza—Miss Bennet," he said.

Gardiner's eyebrows shot up. Had he truly expected that Darcy would not do right by her?

"You will stand by that?" Gardiner asked, his eyes narrowed.

These aspersions on his character were growing more difficult to overlook. "I have said that I will," he said through gritted teeth.

"Wait!" Wickham cried. "Elizabeth is my betrothed. Darcy cannot have her."

Gardiner's jaw dropped open. "Your betrothed?"

"I offered marriage to Elizabeth, and she accepted!" Wickham cried, aggrieved.

Mrs. Gardiner glanced at Elizabeth, who nodded slowly.

Wickham was warming to his indignation. "And then Darcy comes out of nowhere and starts kissing her and…and…other things!"

Darcy was secretly amused that even Wickham could not bring himself to say "held her waist" to the Gardiners.

"Yes, I noticed," Gardiner said dryly. His hard gaze fixed on Darcy again. He clearly viewed Darcy as the enemy here.

"I have a prior claim!" Wickham cried.

Gardiner raised an eyebrow at the younger man. "I will not have my niece haggled over like the last potato at the dinner table." Wickham subsided with a sulky scowl. "The fact of the matter is," Gardiner continued, "that your engagement was not of long standing, having been agreed upon by the principals, what? Only five minutes ago?"

Wickham's head jerked up. "But—!"

"*And* you have not gained my approval or Mr. Bennet's," Gardiner went on more forcefully. Wickham said nothing but glared mutinously at Darcy.

"In the meantime, Mr. Darcy has committed violations upon her person which would make it difficult for Elizabeth to marry anyone else." His formidable stare was turned on Darcy. No doubt Gardiner was aware of stories about men deliberately compromising a woman so she would be forced to marry him. Such situations were rare but not nonexistent. However, they usually involved a penniless gentleman and a lady with a large dowry—and no doubt such incidents often took place with the lady's knowledge and consent. Gardiner frowned, trying to puzzle out why Darcy would deliberately compromise a woman with no prospects, but Elizabeth was worth so much more than any fortune.

"No!" Elizabeth cried, a piteous sound that shriveled Darcy's insides. "No!" The second cry was more forceful. "I did not consent to the-the attack!"

Attack? How could she think of our first kiss that way? It had been a spectacular kiss, and of long duration. Darcy's lips still tingled, and his body retained the impression of Elizabeth pressed against him. Had she not enjoyed it even a little?

Beckett apparently thought the same. "She looked to be returning the kiss," the manservant murmured to the maid. "Didn't you think she was returning it?" She nodded with a barely suppressed smile. Apparently, this was better entertainment than Drury Lane.

Gardiner scowled at his servants and then glared at Darcy. "How can you possibly excuse this abominable behavior?"

Darcy straightened his shoulders, reminding himself that he was still master of Pemberley—even with a bloodstained handkerchief at his lip and a horrified woman staring at him. "I did what was necessary. Miss Bennet cannot marry Mr. Wickham. He is a blackguard of the first order and would ruin her life."

Elizabeth gasped. "So this farce"—she gestured to everyone present—"is to prevent me from marrying George because you hold a grudge against him?"

George? Darcy winced.

"It would seem to me," Mr. Gardiner spoke before Darcy could reply, "that you are the one ruining Miss Bennet's life. She cannot marry Mr. Wickham now that you have compromised her virtue."

Elizabeth gasped. "B-But it was just a kiss…and-and the other…I did not invite his attentions—!"

Her uncle gave her a pitying look. "I know, Lizzy. But you have been compromised before several witnesses."

Realization slowly dawned on Elizabeth's face as she took in the avid gazes of the servants. The Gardiners might be induced to keep quiet about the incident, but nobody could guarantee that the servants would not gossip. If Elizabeth married Wickham and rumors spread, their union would always be tainted by suspicions about her relationship with Darcy.

Which, of course, had been Darcy's intent.

Elizabeth's breath was coming in gasps. "N-No. H-He c-cannot! I will not—!"

Gardiner grimaced and took a few steps toward his niece, putting his hand on her shoulder. "I am sorry, Lizzy. You are far too compromised now to marry anyone else." Darcy wished he felt a greater sense of triumph—or at least relief—at this declaration, but saving her from Wickham meant little if he had forever lost her regard for him.

"No," Elizabeth said miserably.

Gardiner viewed his niece with a sympathetic expression. "It is the way of the world, Lizzy." Darcy bristled at his condescending tone. Yes, Darcy had put her in an impossible position, but she deserved to be treated with honor and dignity.

Once the initial shock had passed, Darcy knew she would see the benefits. She had not expected him to propose; she had not dared to hope. It would take some time to accustom herself to the idea, but the joys of being his wife would smooth away any awkwardness over his initial behavior.

Darcy stepped forward, interposing himself between Elizabeth and her uncle. "Eliz—Miss Bennet, I apologize for the way this has occurred." He tried to appear as contrite as possible, although inside he celebrated the knowledge that she would soon be his. "But will you do me the honor of being my wife?"

Elizabeth burst into tears.

Chapter Seven

This was not the reaction Darcy had dreamed about.

Darcy was at a loss. His first impulse was to enclose her in a comforting embrace, but, of course, such a gesture would not be welcomed. Surely this was just a reaction to the surprise of being kissed in such a way. Soon she would recall their teasing conversations and how much she enjoyed his company. After all, her family had nothing, and any woman in England would give much to become the mistress of Pemberley.

"I do not even like Mr. Darcy!" she wailed.

Any woman except Elizabeth Bennet, apparently.

Darcy's mouth dropped open. Could she possibly be in earnest? She had teased him, laughed with him, danced with him—beautifully. She *liked* him even if she did not *love* him. Did she not?

Elizabeth dried her tears on the sleeve of her gown as her aunt tried awkwardly to embrace her. "I will not marry Mr. Darcy!" she declared.

"Elizabeth—" Darcy pleaded.

She ignored him. "I dislike the man. Why should I marry him?"

Darcy was falling backward into a deep hole, with nothing to grasp to slow or halt his descent. *She* dislikes *me? She dislikes me? But...*

Mr. Gardiner shook his head slowly. "Lizzy, I am afraid you have no choice."

"No!" There was more despair in her tone now.

Darcy had been certain she would embrace the opportunity, at least to help her family if not for her own sake. But even that inducement was not sufficient. The world spun around him. Good Lord, what did she actually think of him?

Gardiner regarded with dissatisfaction the growing crowd of onlookers, which by now included the cook and another maid, no doubt the entire household staff. "Lizzy," he said gently, putting his arm around his niece, "you have had a shock. Perhaps you should go upstairs to rest, and we may discuss this on the morrow over breakfast."

Wickham made a great show of viewing his pocket watch. "I should depart as well. I am expected at the barracks soon." He turned away, oblivious to Elizabeth's despairing look.

The sight broke Darcy's heart. Did she really care for the blackguard?

Gardiner nodded. "I think it would be best." Wickham wasted no time in hurrying back toward the house.

"And you as well, Mr. Darcy." Gardiner gave him a pointed look. "We must discuss this matter another day." In other words, he would cajole his niece into accepting Darcy's offer.

Leave Elizabeth when she was experiencing such distress? Every instinct screamed against it. And he had not achieved his objective of telling Elizabeth the truth about Wickham. Darcy started to voice his objection, but Gardiner spoke over him. "You may return tomorrow if you wish to discuss…the future."

Elizabeth made a noise like a wounded animal, and Darcy's stomach churned even more sickeningly. How could he have misjudged her sentiments so completely?

Darcy nodded to the man and to Elizabeth. "Very well. I will return tomorrow." He gazed into Elizabeth's dark eyes, wishing he could say something to reassure and please her. Wishing he could see some spark of caring in her eyes. But her face was stony as she bit her lip, trying not to cry. Darcy trudged away, his entire body heavy with regret.

***

At this time of year, it grew dark early, but Darcy had not bothered to light any candles in his study. The gradually dimming light suited his mood. The fire had died down, but Darcy had not stirred from his armchair for hours, so the room had grown chilly. He had left orders that nobody disturb him…and now he sat in the chair trying not to think: about Elizabeth, about his egregious assumptions, about the monumental errors that had brought events to this head. Sleep would be the best remedy, but he feared dreams populated by Elizabeth.

His thoughts turned in circles like a dog chasing its tail. Where had he first gone wrong? Was it at the Meryton assembly? Or was it when he left Hertfordshire without declaring his feelings for Elizabeth? Perhaps it was his failure to warn Elizabeth immediately about the danger that Wickham posed.

No. He was deluding himself if he thought anything was to blame except for his arrogant assumption that she returned his attraction. If he had suspected Elizabeth harbored reservations, he had assumed her doubts would be quelled by his fortune.

Both his hands clenched into fists. Whatever he had done, however he had arrived at this place, Darcy was certainly guilty of ruining both of their lives.

By compromising her, Darcy had inevitably tied their lives together. Tied his life to a woman who did not want him. He could tolerate ruining his own life; after all, it was his to ruin. But being the instrument of destroying the life of the woman he loved…

That thought seemed to crush his lungs in an iron grip, making it difficult to breath.

That was the point when he usually gave up on thinking altogether. Or attempted to.

Without so much as a knock, the door was flung open. Light flooded in from the hallway. Darcy started and then twisted around in his chair to growl at whoever was disobeying his orders. Georgiana stood in the doorway with his cousin, Richard Fitzwilliam, behind her.

This did not bode well. They could not be as easily deterred as servants.

Darcy turned back toward the fire without a word, but they ignored the hint. Their footfalls were muffled by the carpet as they approached his chair. Georgiana spoke to Richard as if Darcy were not in the room. "He has been holed up in here for hours. Not working. Not reading. Not even lighting the candles."

Richard leaned over to scrutinize his cousin, his face inches from Darcy's. A move designed to provoke a reaction, which it did. With a hand on his chest, Darcy forcefully pushed his cousin away. A corner of Richard's mouth curved upward as he addressed Georgiana. "It is good you sent for me. Will you light the candles? I shall get a blaze started."

Remaining immobile, Darcy watched as his cousin stacked wood on the dying embers and coaxed flames into life. Damnation. Summoning Richard had been a clever thought. Darcy could have ignored Georgiana and ordered her to leave him alone; she was still the younger sister. But experience had taught Darcy that Richard would not suffer being ignored.

Once the candles were lit and a fire was warming the room, Richard strolled to the sideboard and poured a glass of port. Handing it to Darcy, he instructed, "Drink it all."

Getting foxed sounded like a capital idea to Darcy, so he consumed it in three gulps and held out his glass for more. However, no more port was forthcoming, and Darcy did not have the energy to obtain it of his own accord.

Instead, Georgiana and Richard took seats on either side of his chair, bracketing him in. "Darcy, can you tell me what is the matter?" Richard asked gently.

"Everything is fine, Richard. Go away."

Richard rolled his eyes at Georgiana. "You did not warn me that he would sound like a sulky child."

"Earlier he would not speak at all," she countered. "This is progress. I pray you, continue."

"I will not depart until you speak with me," Richard warned Darcy. "You might as well concede defeat now."

Darcy continued to stare at the fire. "I have no need or desire for conversation."

Richard leaned back in his chair. "Very well. I shall converse with Georgiana." Darcy's sister chuckled. "I pray you, fair cousin, tell me in great detail about your last shopping trip with my mother. Did you purchase a new hat?"

Georgiana immediately caught on to his scheme. "I did indeed," she said with a grin. "It is blue, although Aunt Mary thought the green would suit me better. But I loved the feathers in the blue hat. Then I found the most exquisite lace. I thought it too dear, but Aunt Mary said I would not find such fine lace again in my lifetime, so I should purchase it while I could. I believe I will have it affixed to the new gown I am having made up for the dinner at the Randalls'. Or perhaps I will save it to be part of a ball gown for my coming out year. It really is so fine! Then we went to Madame Ballard's shop, and she had the daintiest gloves in a white kidskin—"

Darcy's patience was worn out. "Enough!" he bellowed. Georgiana giggled; they were enjoying themselves a little too much.

"Are you prepared to tell us what happened, or shall I torture you with details about dancing slippers?" she asked. When Darcy did not respond, she leaned forward anxiously. "Does this have to do with Miss Bennet?"

Darcy sighed at the sound of her name. Perhaps appearing to cooperate would be the best way to encourage their departure. "Very well, I will tell you." Perhaps a few vague statements would satisfy them.

However, once Darcy started the story, the words tumbled out of his mouth faster and faster. Soon he had confessed all: his feelings for Elizabeth, Wickham's threats, and the entire disaster at the Gardiners' house.

When his story faltered to a conclusion, the room was silent.

"I am impressed," Richard said slowly. "When you make a mistake you do so thoroughly. No half measures for you."

Darcy snorted despite himself.

Georgiana's hand covered her mouth, and her eyes were wide with horror as if she witnessed a battlefield littered with dead soldiers. "You *kissed* her? Before her aunt and uncle and the servants?"

"And Wickham," Richard added helpfully.

"I could think of nothing else to do," Darcy confessed.

Richard drew his brows together. "Did you consider calmly telling her the story of Georgiana's experience with Wickham and requesting that she break off the engagement?"

No, it had not occurred to Darcy. Not even hours later. He shook his head. "It was too late for such explanations. She had already *accepted* him."

Richard made an impatient noise. "I am certain that any woman who could secure your regard would have listened to your explanations."

Yes, Darcy thought miserably, staring into his empty glass. *She probably would have listened.*

Georgiana threw her hands in the air. "It is not as if Mr. Wickham would have married her that instant. You would have had time to convince her of the truth! She could have broken off the engagement later."

"I-I—" Darcy sputtered.

"You panicked," Richard supplied.

Darcy tipped his head back, resting it on the back of his chair. "I suppose I did. All I could think was that I could not allow Wickham to steal her away and ruin her life." He stared at the ceiling. "I also believed she would be happy—or at least content—to marry me. I thought she at least..." His voice trailed off, unable to finish the sentence.

Richard stood and strolled to the window, gazing out even though there was nothing to see in the darkness. "So you are engaged to a woman who does not like you."

Darcy closed his eyes briefly. "Worse. I do not know if I am engaged to her at all." Richard gave him a quizzical look. "She did not agree to the engagement. Nor did she break off her promise to Wickham."

Richard shook his head slowly. "Good Lord, it just keeps getting worse."

Darcy continued, "I went to Gracechurch Street with the purpose of telling her the whole story, but I never had the opportunity."

Georgiana's hand flew to her mouth. "Might he convince her to elope with him?"

Darcy experienced a jolt of panic but then shook his head. "I do not know what his purpose was in offering marriage, but I cannot imagine he intended to follow through. Most likely he was only attempting to thwart me."

Richard leaned his shoulder against the wall, his arms crossed as he frowned in thought. "It seems to me the first object is to convince Miss Bennet of Wickham's perfidy. At the very least that would insulate her from the danger of marrying him. Have you considered writing her a letter? You could hardly do *worse* expressing yourself in writing."

"I thank you for that endorsement, Cuz," Darcy sneered at him. "But I did have a note sent round to the Gardiners'."

"And?" Georgiana asked breathlessly.

Darcy sighed heavily. "Her uncle returned the letter unopened with a note saying she would not accept a letter from a man to whom she is not related."

"Oh." Georgiana winced.

Darcy sighed. "What am I to do?"

"You could write to her uncle with the story about Wickham. Gardiner could hardly refuse to read your letter, and he is not likely to dismiss it out of hand." Richard straightened to his full height. "Allow me to deliver the letter. I can vouch for the veracity."

Georgiana lifted her head. "I have an even better idea." Darcy's eyebrows rose. His sister was usually reserved when discussing Wickham; he was surprised she had not already fled the room.

"I will go to visit Elizabeth Bennet," she announced.

"That is an excellent idea!" Richard cried.

They both sought Darcy's approbation. He had doubts about the wisdom of stirring up old memories for his sister, but she would rebel if he treated her like a child. "A happy thought, Georgiana. I thank you."

His sense of relief mingled with uncertainty. Speaking with Georgiana should extinguish whatever feelings Elizabeth had for Wickham, but it would not solve the larger problem: Elizabeth did not love Darcy.

Chapter Eight

"Would you like another cup of tea, Lizzy?" Aunt Gardiner asked.

Elizabeth shook her head mutely as she stared unseeing out of the window. Her aunt had insisted that she stay in bed to recover from the shock of the previous day's events, although Elizabeth would much rather be pacing, or perhaps taking a long walk.

"I put extra sugar in it," her aunt said enticingly.

Elizabeth sighed and took the cup, placing it on the table beside her bed. Her aunt was of the opinion that enough tea could solve anything, including nervous conditions, a broken heart, a fever, the plague—and, most likely, the Peninsular War. Elizabeth had already consumed so much tea that morning she felt as if she would float away.

Despite all the tea, she remained mired in an odd state of anger mixed with sadness, a dollop of guilt, and a pinch of shame: a recipe for a particularly awful stew. The anger was directed at Mr. Darcy for his high-handed behavior and arrogant assumption that naturally she would prefer him over Mr. Wickham because of his fortune.

The sadness had been provoked by a realization during her long, sleepless night that she could not marry Mr. Wickham; any future relationship between them would forever be tainted by Mr. Darcy's actions. If Elizabeth loved Mr. Wickham, perhaps they could overcome that obstacle, but her amiable feelings toward him were not enough to surmount the scandal which could erupt if she defied Mr. Darcy.

She had sent him a note that morning breaking off the engagement. Hopefully her mother would not be angry that she had declined another eligible offer of marriage. Of course, if her mother knew Elizabeth intended to refuse Mr. Darcy…

The guilt sprang from that intended refusal. Mr. Darcy could provide even more security to her mother and sisters, but Elizabeth could not imagine accepting his offer. She was too angry, and he was too selfish and disdainful of others.

And the shame stemmed from that small (very small, Elizabeth insisted to herself) part of her soul which seemed content—even delighted—at the prospect of marrying Mr. Darcy. Feeling like a traitor to her own values and identity, she had at first attempted to deny such sentiments. How could the thought of a future with that man provoke anything other than revulsion?

But in the stillness of the nighttime, Elizabeth had admitted to herself that even before the incident in the garden, she had caught herself admiring his fine figure and serious manner. And then the kiss…well, the kiss…

Elizabeth always found herself distracted when she recalled the kiss. It had been very… Extremely…

Surely she would not have responded so…passionately if she had been prepared for the kiss. And it was her first real kiss; any previous kisses had been mere meetings of the lips by comparison. Of course, she had a strong reaction.

Perhaps all real kisses were like that. Did all wives feel like their husband's kisses were a drug that they craved every minute of every day? Elizabeth somehow doubted it. Her mother certainly seemed more preoccupied by her nerves than her husband's lips. And her aunt did not appear to crave her uncle's touch.

If a simple kiss could engender such sensations, what would happen in the marital bed? Elizabeth shivered, goosebumps erupting along her arms. How would it feel if Mr. Darcy touched her?

Nor was the effect limited to his kisses. Conversation with the man always had a vivacity and energy she experienced with nobody else. Although he was proud and difficult, she always enjoyed matching wits with him. Unfortunately, her conversations with Mr. Wickham could not compare; he was amiable and pleasant, but he never made her feel quite so alive.

And, thus, the shame.

"You are thinking about Mr. Darcy again?" Aunt Gardiner asked, sitting on the side of Elizabeth's bed.

"How did you know?"

Her aunt smiled gently, sadly. "You develop a small crease here whenever you are worrying the subject." She indicated with a finger to her own forehead.

Elizabeth sat up straighter in bed. "I do not know if I can reconcile myself to becoming his wife."

"It is despicable the way he took advantage of you, but too often that is the way of the world. Wealthy men believe they are entitled to…privileges," Aunt Gardiner spat out the words, leaving no doubt of her disapproval.

"He simply assumed I would be happy to be his wife!"

"It is not an unreasonable assumption. Most women would be thrilled to become the mistress of Pemberley."

"They may have him."

Aunt Gardiner leaned forward and took Elizabeth's hand in hers. "Being Mrs. Darcy would have many compensations. Once you had an heir and a spare, you need not be intimate—"Elizabeth did not allow her aunt to finish. Pulling her hand from her aunt's grasp, she clutched the bed covers instead. "Why does everyone assume I will simply marry him? There are always choices...."

The other woman's brows drew together. "What else would you do?"

"I-I could refuse to marry anyone. I could become a nun!"

Her aunt's lips twitched. "That is a possibility I had not considered....You are not known for your...piety." Elizabeth could not refute that accusation. "Would that be truly preferable to marrying Mr. Darcy? After all, he is very wealthy. He could help your family tremendously."

"I know." Elizabeth forced herself to release her grip on the covers.

The back of her head throbbed, threatening to become a headache. Was Elizabeth's attraction to the man a result of his wealth rather than genuine feelings? She had not loved Mr. Wickham, but she had been willing to marry him because of his many merits. Was she now perceiving merits in Mr. Darcy because she found his fortune attractive? Elizabeth had no desire to form a marital bond under such pretext.

She sipped her cooling—and far too sweet—tea. How did Mr. Darcy so constantly confuse her? Even her own thoughts and desires confounded her.

Perhaps she should not have returned his note unopened. But sending a letter as if they were already engaged had seemed presumptuous on his part. She had been seriously tempted to throw it in the fireplace; however, her uncle had believed she should return it. Now she wished she knew the letter's contents. She rubbed the back of her neck, trying to loosen tense muscles.

Lying in bed would not solve her dilemma. Elizabeth pulled back the covers and swung her legs over the side of the bed. "I believe I shall take a walk. Perhaps that will clear my head."

Her aunt stood. "It may do you good. I will leave you to dress."

But before she reached the door, it opened, and Shaw peered in. "If you please, ma'am, there's a Miss Darcy here to see Miss Bennet."

Elizabeth's eyes widened. "Miss Darcy?" The girl must be there to plead her brother's case.

She knew little about Mr. Darcy's sister other than her age. Mr. Wickham had described her as proud and arrogant, and Elizabeth pictured a younger version of Miss Bingley. The very thought made her head pound.

Aunt Gardiner must have guessed her thoughts from her expression. She pursed her lips. "Hopefully the sister is less difficult than the brother. I shall go down and greet Miss Darcy, so you will have time to dress."

"Thank you," Elizabeth said softly.

***

Twenty minutes later, Elizabeth was in the Gardiners' drawing room with Miss Darcy seated opposite her—and yet another cup of tea in front of her. Aunt Gardiner had slipped out of the drawing room to report that the girl was quiet, well-mannered, and exceedingly shy. Despite her nervousness, however, she seemed determined to speak with Elizabeth. Now that Elizabeth was facing the girl, she agreed with her aunt's assessment; there was no air of arrogance or superiority about her. Why had Mr. Wickham described her otherwise?

Her aunt had offered to remain in the drawing room, but Miss Darcy had appeared more at ease with Elizabeth alone, so she had declined. They exchanged pleasantries about the weather and the upcoming Christmas holiday. Elizabeth learned that most of the Darcys' relatives were away from town for the Christmas season. She was also informed that Mr. Darcy gave his sister Christmas gifts which were far more than she deserved, and that he was very good at snapdragon while Miss Darcy preferred charades.

The girl's hands fidgeted with the sash of her dress, and she swallowed frequently. Elizabeth wondered if the girl would ever work up the nerve to move beyond small talk. Finally, when there was a lull in the conversation, Miss Darcy seized the opportunity. She lifted her chin and looked Elizabeth in the eye. "I must speak to you about M-Mr. Wickham."

Elizabeth's eyebrows rose. She had expected a stalwart defense of Mr. Darcy rather than stories about Mr. Wickham. After all, Miss Darcy must have been quite young when Mr. Wickham had left Pemberley.

Miss Darcy continued without prompting. "I know my brother warned you about Mr. Wickham's character, but he did not give you specific reasons for caution…out of a sense of delicacy for my feelings."

Her feelings? How did anything concerning Mr. Wickham affect Miss Darcy?

The girl held herself very still, looking quite small on the upholstered settee. "But I believe you should know the whole story, so you will understand William's concerns and actions."

And she proceeded to relate to Elizabeth a most amazing tale of how Mr. Wickham had rejected the living set aside for him in Mr. Darcy's will. Instead, he had received a payment in cash, which he wasted on a life of idleness and dissipation. Then he had concocted a scheme to seduce and marry Georgiana to gain access to her dowry.

"If William had not arrived at Ramsgate unexpectedly, Mr. Wickham would certainly have persuaded me to elope with him—for I did believe myself in love with him," Miss Darcy said, her voice trembling a little. "But when my brother turned him away, Mr. Wickham left Ramsgate altogether, and I knew William was right. If he had truly loved me, he would have continued trying to win my hand, or he would have been willing to wait until I was older. But when William opposed the match, he gave up the scheme and went into the army." Tears glistened in the girl's eyes. "He never really loved me; it was all playacting."

Her chest aching in sympathy, Elizabeth was struck by this girl's courage at relating such a story—which did not show her in a favorable light and could ruin her reputation if generally known—to a complete stranger. Miss Darcy must love her brother very much to take such risks.

Elizabeth crossed the distance between them in two steps and, with a rustle of petticoats, sank onto the settee next to the girl. Miss Darcy had been fumbling about, seeking her handkerchief, so Elizabeth handed the girl hers. She accepted it and gingerly wiped her eyes. "I beg your pardon. I am not usually such a watering pot," Miss Darcy said with a shaky laugh.

"I can imagine recalling such events is most distressing," Elizabeth said in a low, soothing voice. She wanted to put her arms around the girl and comfort her, but their brief acquaintance did not allow such liberties.

Miss Darcy peered at Elizabeth through tear-spangled lashes. "Do you believe me?"

Elizabeth blinked several times in rapid succession. Disbelieving the story had not even occurred to her; she had only thought of alleviating the younger woman's distress. There was no guile or deceit in Miss Darcy's manner. It was nigh inconceivable that she had concocted such a shameful story.

But if Elizabeth accepted the truth of Miss Darcy's story, she would be forced to admit that Mr. Wickham had lied to her about Mr. Darcy, his family, and many of his interactions with the man. Furthermore, Mr. Wickham had attempted to take the innocence of a girl of fifteen years for no other reason than his own personal gain.

Elizabeth suddenly felt dizzy, as if she had been spinning in circles and the world swirled around her. This was the man she had believed in. This was the man she had agreed to marry. This was the man she had nearly entrusted with her heart and entire future.

Elizabeth clutched the arm of the settee as if it were the only solid thing in the room. Mr. Darcy had warned her, but she had not credited his words. Confident in her own discernment, she had chosen to believe Mr. Wickham instead. Elizabeth now saw that there were inconsistencies in Mr. Wickham's accounts of himself that she had willingly ignored. And she had discounted how eager he had been to relay personal stories and to slander Mr. Darcy's name. Yes, he was at fault, but so was she. He had poured his poison into a willing ear.

Why was I so eager to believe the worst of Mr. Darcy? Just because he had mortified my vanity at the Meryton assembly? How petty her actions appeared to her now. Elizabeth was buffeted by a whirlwind, pulled down and down and unable to know which way was up.

"Y-Yes, of course," Elizabeth responded to Miss Darcy rather absently, torn between self-recriminations and horror at Mr. Wickham's behavior. Her hand rose to cover her mouth as if she could somehow reclaim all the terrible things she had said to Mr. Darcy throughout their acquaintance. Miss Darcy had held up a mirror to Elizabeth's own actions, and Elizabeth did not like her reflection at all. The other woman regarded her with no small alarm; Elizabeth must appear quite pale and agitated.

"You do believe me?" Miss Darcy repeated in a plaintive voice. Her eyes were practically begging Elizabeth.

Elizabeth swallowed, trying to focus on her rather distressed guest. "Yes, Miss Darcy, I do." She grasped and squeezed the girl's hand. "I am simply aghast at my own lack of judgment."

Miss Darcy squeezed back. "He deceived me as well, and I knew his character. I had far more reason for suspicion than you."

"Do not chastise yourself," Elizabeth told her. "You were very young."

The girl took Elizabeth's other hand and turned to face her completely, her eyes shining with hope. "If you believe me, will you accept William's offer of marriage?"

Taken off guard, Elizabeth opened her mouth to respond and then closed it again. If she believed Miss Darcy and accepted that she had been completely deceived about Mr. Wickham's character, then Elizabeth must also be prepared to believe that she had been completely wrong in her assessment of Mr. Darcy. This realization plunged her back into the whirlwind. *I have been wrong about Mr. Wickham and wrong about Mr. Darcy. What else have I been wrong about?* Perhaps Mr. Bingley was secretly tyrannical, and Mr. Collins was Prince Charming. It was almost too much to comprehend.

However, accepting that her opinion of Mr. Darcy was mistaken was not the same thing as wishing to marry the man. After a moment's reflection, Elizabeth responded slowly to the other woman, "It is not quite that simple…"

"Of course not!" Miss Darcy exclaimed. "He described how he kissed you before your aunt and uncle's entire household. I would be mortified." Her eyes were almost as round as her mouth.

Elizabeth simply nodded, viewing these actions in a new light.

"But let me assure you that my brother is the best of men," Miss Darcy rattled on. "Everyone says so. The servants love him, and he has the happiest tenants in Derbyshire. And, of course, he is a wonderful older brother; sometimes he is kind to me even when I do not deserve it."

Elizabeth was a little amused at the younger sister singing her brother's praises. Lydia would certainly never be caught saying such laudatory words about Elizabeth! "It is a complicated situation," Elizabeth explained. "I did not expect his…proposal." *To put it mildly.* "We are not very well acquainted."

Miss Darcy clasped her hands together as if in supplication. "But you *must* marry him!"

Bracing herself for another argument about how her reputation had been compromised, Elizabeth reached for her teacup and took a sip to disguise her inevitable wince.

"He is violently in love with you."

Elizabeth barely managed not to spray tea all over the front of her dress. She set down the cup with shaking hands before replying. Surely Miss Darcy must be wrong. She had misinterpreted her brother's words. He had compromised Elizabeth to save her from Mr. Wickham, but she had seen no sign of his particular regard for her. "In love...with me? W-Why do you say so?"

"He told me so."

Perhaps the girl was simply being carried away by her sense of romance. "What did he say?"

"He told me he had admired you since he first saw you in Hertfordshire, and he feared Mr. Wickham would propose to you to get revenge on him. He is always searching for ways to hurt William."

Elizabeth's world was turned upside down once again. Mr. Wickham had not proposed because he cared for her, but to get revenge on Mr. Darcy. She had nearly become a tool for his revenge. But such a plot would not succeed if Mr. Darcy did not actually care for Elizabeth. It followed, therefore, that not only did Mr. Darcy have feelings for her but also Mr. Wickham recognized them.

It made sense in a twisted way; many pieces of the puzzle fell into place. She had wondered if Mr. Wickham was truly in love with her but could not conceive another motive for proposing. Her dowry certainly would not entice him.

Mr. Darcy loved her, and Mr. Wickham did not. *Have I been wrong in my understanding of everyone's feelings? Perhaps Jane secretly loathes me, and Miss Bingley actually holds me in the greatest esteem.*

"Are you feeling ill?" Miss Darcy asked suddenly. "You have grown quite pale."

Elizabeth could only imagine.

"Maybe you should drink more tea." The girl reached for Elizabeth's teacup.

"No," Elizabeth said, managing a calm voice. "I am heartily sick of tea. I thank you, Miss Darcy. I do not feel ill. I simply...was not prepared for this news."

The girl drew back her hand. "Mr. Wickham's behavior is quite shocking. I am sorry you had to hear that story."

Oddly, the news of Mr. Darcy's sentiments may have shaken Elizabeth even more than Mr. Wickham's perfidy. "I am glad you informed me," Elizabeth murmured.

"Perhaps you should rest?" the girl asked.

Elizabeth glanced down at her trembling hands. "Yes, perhaps I should."

"I would like to visit again. If you do not mind?" Miss Darcy asked shyly.

Once she moved past her initial reserve, the girl was pleasant company. Elizabeth could imagine becoming her friend. "Yes, I would like that."

It would be nice to see a friendly face again after what was sure to be a series of long, sleepless nights.

Chapter Nine

After half an hour of futile efforts to read a book, Elizabeth was forced to concede that rest was not what she needed. She was…dazed, as if she had discovered the color she had known all her life as green was actually yellow or that the disc that rose in the morning was really called the moon. She was disoriented; never before had her own discernment deserted her so completely.

Ashamed of her own lack of judgment and mindful of the need to keep Miss Darcy's secret, she only told the Gardiners that the sister had pleaded the brother's case. *If only Jane were here!* Elizabeth would have gladly confided in her sister.

Her thoughts bounced around inside her head, slipping from wonder at Mr. Darcy to anger at Mr. Wickham to anxiety about what the future held. She did not know what would happen, and worse, she was not sure what she wanted to have happen. It was most unsettling for someone who always prided herself on her clarity of thinking.

What she needed was a walk to clear her mind. There was a park not far from Gracechurch Street where Elizabeth often strolled, but she had not visited it for two days. She donned her walking boots and pelisse—fortunately the weather continued mild—informed her aunt of her plans, and set off at a brisk pace.

After only a few steps, she sensed someone coming up behind her. Turning her head, she found Mr. Darcy. "Would you be so good as to allow me to accompany you on your walk today?" His face was a still mask, revealing nothing of his thoughts.

Unbidden, memories arose: the insult at the Meryton assembly, the sneers at Netherfield, the unwanted kiss in the garden--and the astonishing idea that he actually loved Elizabeth. Could Miss Darcy possibly be correct?

"I suppose I cannot prevent you," she retorted without breaking stride.

Mr. Darcy winced but hurried to match her pace. They were silent until they reached the edge of the park, where Elizabeth slowed to a more leisurely stroll. When it became apparent she would not initiate a conversation, Mr. Darcy finally cleared his throat. "Georgiana was pleased to have the opportunity to meet you."

Elizabeth stared straight ahead. "She is a most amiable girl."

"I am pleased you enjoyed each other's company." He was silent for a moment. Distant city noises intruded upon Elizabeth's consciousness, accompanied by the soft scrape of their shoes on the stone pathway. "She was under the impression that you took her story to heart."

"I did." Thank goodness they were walking, and she need not meet his eyes! "It pains me that I was so deceived as to Mr. Wickham's character."

His eyes were fixed on the pathway. "I am sorry to be the occasion of any pain."

"It is preferable to ignorance."

"Do you understand now the reasons for my actions yesterday?"

Elizabeth stumbled and almost fell but caught herself before Mr. Darcy's assistance was necessary. "I understand why you believed you needed to prevent my engagement to Mr. Wickham." The memory of that shameful event brought heat to her face. "But I do not see the necessity for taking such inappropriate actions," she snapped.

Mr. Darcy recoiled at the vehemence of her reaction. "I did not believe— I thought I must—" He made a frustrated noise in the back of his throat and adjusted his hat nervously. "I cannot apologize enough for my untoward behavior. The truth, Miss Bennet, is that I panicked. I was not thinking rationally, and I can only beg you to forgive me."

This confession left her speechless. How had such a proud man left himself so vulnerable to her scorn and rejection? Could she trust in his sincerity? She stopped abruptly to scrutinize his face, but she saw no guile in his countenance. His brow furrowed as he withstood her examination. "Panicked?" she echoed.

He fidgeted, yanking at the ruffles at his cuff as if they were responsible for his current agitation. "I was afraid," he admitted, his gaze fixed over her shoulder. "I thought you would be lost to me forever."

What? He actually believed... He truly feared losing me that much? And he willingly confesses it to me? The dazed sensation returned in force.

Despite Miss Darcy's claim, Elizabeth had not quite credited the idea that he harbored a passionate attachment for her. While it did explain the desperate kiss in the garden, it was difficult to reconcile with all the times he had stared at her in disapproval or made sneering comments. When you loved someone, were you not supposed to be nice to them? Although if she viewed it through a different lens, perhaps...

Was it possible that he had been staring because he admired her? Or that his comments had been meant to be teasing rather than insulting? Truthfully most of the worst comments had been made by Miss Bingley and Mrs. Hurst; Elizabeth had just assumed he agreed with them.

It was true that he had not avoided her company when she had visited Netherfield. He frequently engaged her in conversation, and he had sought her as a dance partner at the Netherfield ball. Perhaps he did feel enough affection for her…Perhaps he did love her enough that the prospect of her engagement to Mr. Wickham would drive him to desperate action.

What courage he must possess to kiss her without knowing her feelings! To kiss her knowing that mortification was the inevitable result! And he was such a proper man, so aware of everyone's judgment.

Elizabeth felt as if she had just opened her eyes and that previously unnoticed vistas had suddenly appeared before her.

But did she really want to explore this new territory?

The answer would have been no if Mr. Darcy had been the man she thought he was, but this other Mr. Darcy…

Oh. Elizabeth realized she was staring at him as they stood in the middle of the pathway. Their faces were only a foot apart, raising uncomfortable memories of their kiss yesterday. How had they managed to move so close to each other? Elizabeth colored and shuffled backward a few steps. In all her previous encounters with the man, Elizabeth had been certain how she should respond to him, but this new Mr. Darcy confused and vexed her.

"Can you find it in your heart to forgive my most grievous error?" His voice was quite plaintive.

Elizabeth considered as Mr. Darcy squirmed under the scrutiny of her gaze. Although she could not approve of the method he had used to separate her from Mr. Wickham, she understood it. He had been acting from the best intentions. He was penitent and desirous of her forgiveness. "Yes, of course, I forgive you."

Immediately his body loosened, and he stood a little taller. Still, anxiety etched lines into his face, and she found herself wishing to give him some reassurance—some token that she might someday be favorably disposed toward him. "I am not…" Unable to bear the weight of his stare, Elizabeth turned her eyes to the park, staring at brown grass and bare tree limbs. She swallowed. "I am not lost to you." His breath caught. "I…sent Mr. Wickham a note this morning informing him that I do not believe we may continue the engagement."

Mr. Darcy sighed, and his body relaxed even more. "I am…relieved to hear that." The tentative expression on his face suggested he wanted to discuss the state of their courtship, but Elizabeth was not equal to that conversation. She swung back toward the pathway and resumed walking.

Mr. Darcy fell into step beside her. Several minutes passed in which the silence between them grew uncomfortable. He had not offered Elizabeth his arm, and she was acutely aware that the pace between them was disjointed and uneven.

She glanced at his profile, stern and unforgiving. He was staring at the park as if it had somehow offended him. Was he angry that she had not immediately accepted his offer?

Finally, she could bear the silence no longer. "It is pleasant to have such mild weather this time of year," she said with a sportive grin.

He was startled out of his reverie. "Hmm? Oh yes."

Another silence stretched between them.

"Do you believe we shall have rain?"

He glanced at the faded blue winter sky. "I do not imagine so."

"Snow then?"

He blinked. "No."

"Hail?"

His lips twitched.

"No."

"A blizzard perhaps?"

He huffed a laugh. "I do not believe that is likely."

"Perhaps a plague of locusts?"

He slid her a sidelong glance. "I do not believe that could properly be considered a weather event."

She shrugged. "Well, Mama always says I should discuss the weather when all else fails, but it appears I have no more weather to discuss."

He snorted, then drew a deep breath. "I hope your willingness to discuss the weather is an indication that you are not too terribly angry at my presumption."

There was another long silence. The path curved, taking them along the bank of a pond.

"Not terribly angry, but still somewhat angry," she replied. He nodded his understanding. "So how did you come to be outside my uncle's house just as I was departing? I find that a happy coincidence.

"Er…" He licked his lips, glancing around the park before answering. "I…ah…was lingering outside…on the street…hoping you would leave the house." He shrugged sheepishly. "Your uncle's neighbors gave me some puzzled looks."

He must have wanted to speak with her quite desperately. "For how long?"

Was he blushing? "Not so long. I arrived this morning."

"At what time?"

He was suddenly, intensely interested in a duck paddling in the pond. "At about seven or so."

"Seven?" It was now close to noon! And Mr. Darcy was a busy man.

He shrugged. "I did not want to miss an opportunity to talk with you."

She could not prevent a smile. "It is customary if one wishes to speak with a person to knock on the door. It does offer a certain efficiency."

"I did not know if you would receive me." His face was stony.

There was that. Elizabeth might not have spoken with him before Miss Darcy's visit, but now…

She took some time before replying. "After your sister's visit, I realized that our acquaintance has been one long comedy of errors. I have not acquired a good understanding of your character or conduct, and I daresay you have not received a complete picture of mine."

"No. I—" He spoke as if each word rubbed his throat raw. "Before…In the garden….I believed you…recognized my attentions for what they were, and you welcomed them."

This admission must have been difficult to make. Elizabeth fought a most ridiculous and inappropriate impulse to hug him. How her reaction yesterday must have hurt him! She had stabbed him and twisted the knife without realizing it.

And the fault was hers. She had allowed her own prejudice toward the man to cloud her normally good insight into people. "Apparently, I am too obtuse for a subtle approach, Mr. Darcy. You would have done better to hit me over the head."

He smiled. "I would not wish to injure you."

She found herself smiling in return. "You could use a bouquet of flowers."

His lips were pressed together, suppressing a laugh. "That would be quite messy and a waste of perfectly good flowers."

"And I suppose it would be rather confusing without any kind of explanation. Very well, forget that idea. I shall remain a hopeless case."

"Do not say that," he murmured in a tone so strangled that Elizabeth glanced at him in alarm. He took a step toward her. "I alone created this catastrophe. I alone should suffer for it."

She was shaking her head before he finished speaking. "You are not alone, and I am not blameless. I misjudged you badly."

He lifted his head and stared into her eyes, his lips parted slightly. "I pray you, tell me I am not too late. That I can unwind the damage I have done to your estimation of me."

This poignant plea struck a chord deep within Elizabeth's chest. No woman could fail to be moved by such a request. However, her feelings for Mr. Darcy were hopelessly tangled by now. Freed of obligations to Mr. Wickham, Elizabeth could finally admit her attraction to Mr. Darcy, but he had mortified her in the garden the previous day. Would he always be so high-handed? Was it really possible that such a man could be violently in love with her? It seemed inconceivable. But he was behaving much as a suitor would, and there could be no possible motive for him to pretend an admiration for her that he did not feel.

Nor could she imagine another motive to kiss her the way he had. He did have a feud with Wickham, but surely he would not sacrifice his own marital happiness for its sake.

"You are not too late," she assured him. He breathed out a sigh of relief. "But I am confused, Mr. Darcy. My aunt and uncle insist that I have no choice other than to marry you after your actions yesterday." He had the grace to blush. "Do you believe differently?"

He looked out over the pond, his expression pensive. "At the time of the kiss, I believed you would welcome the opportunity to become my wife, and that would persuade you to overlook the...unusual circumstances of my proposal. I *am* hoping to persuade you to marry me, which would avert any scandal. But if not...Perhaps I could pay off the servants..." He did not seem happy at that prospect.

"I told my aunt I would consider a convent."

A side of his mouth lifted in a half-smile. "I hope I can persuade you that life with me would be preferable." He took a step closer to her.

An errant breeze wafted his sandalwood scent toward her, a scent she had always enjoyed. "I hope I can persuade you that life with me could be very good indeed." His voice had grown husky and deep, setting something humming inside Elizabeth.

His eyes, darkened with desire, locked on hers, mesmerizing her. She could not pull her gaze from his. At that moment she had no difficulty imagining how good life with him could be.

The tip of his tongue moistened his lips, prompting memories of the kiss in the garden. It had been…transcendent.

Her fingers itched to touch him…to stroke the softness of his hair…to feel the hard planes of his chest and measure the width of his shoulders with her hands. These desires took her off guard. She had never experienced this heady rush of sensations with any other man. Even Mr. Wickham—who had been pleasant and good company—had never required her to restrain herself from reaching out to touch him. However, there was far more to a marriage than desire. Could she be happy with such a proud, difficult man? A man who expected the world to bend to his will?

Mr. Darcy's handsome features were distracting, impeding Elizabeth's rational thoughts. She averted her eyes to the tips of her shoes peeking out from the hem of her dress.

"Elizabeth?" His question had a tinge of anxiety in it.

"Your sister"—her throat closed up, and she needed to start again—"your sister is under the impression that you are a little in love with me."

He shook his head. "No, Miss Bennet, I am not a little in love with you." For some reason she did not want to examine, Elizabeth's heart sank at this news. It should come as a relief, but instead she was irrationally disappointed—as if she had, in a short time, come to rely upon the idea that he loved her.

Mr. Darcy continued, "I am violently, irrevocably, passionately in love with you and have been since before my party quitted Netherfield."

Oh. Her breath caught. *Well, that declaration left little room for doubt.*

Still, he could be deceiving himself. His passion could be transitory and easily lost. Could she tie her future to a hope?

She had been grievously mistaken about Mr. Wickham's character and was now doubly uncertain about her own judgment. On the other hand, he could be of enormous help to her family. Could she afford to decline his offer?

"Forgive me, Mr. Darcy, but I"—she swallowed—"I do not understand why you have singled me out for the honor of your attention when there are undoubtedly many other women who have been vying for your favor."

He gasped. "Do you not see yourself?" he asked in wonder. "From the first moment I saw you in the assembly hall, your light shone so brightly that it eclipsed every other woman—every other person—present."

Elizabeth's heart swelled at his words, and yet… "There are many pretty women in the world. Why do you single me out?"

His hand raised, and his fingers skimmed lightly over her cheek. She held her breath. "I do not simply crave your beauty. I crave the power of your mind. Your wit. Your conversation. When I speak with other women about moral failings, they say, 'Ah yes, sir, you have the right of it.' But when I speak to Elizabeth Bennet, you say, 'Do you consider vanity and pride to be failings?' and then you argue with me." His hand cupped her cheek, and his thumb gently brushed over her lips.

Her breathing was becoming more ragged. "You like that I argue with you?"

His smile was gentle. "I do. It is something that I did not know I needed. But I need it, desperately."

Elizabeth gasped, struggling to keep her eyes fixed on his. Such ardor threatened to overwhelm her senses.

"I want to enjoy the power of that mind, that wit, and that conversation for the rest of my life," he continued. "It is the missing piece of my life that I did not know was missing. It is the thing that I did not know I was searching for. All these years I have been dissatisfied with my marital choices and despaired of ever finding a woman who made my heart race and my soul sing."

Elizabeth was speechless for perhaps the first time in her life. But how could she possibly respond to such eloquence, such intensity? He had effectively obliterated any doubts she had that he loved her, but they had been replaced with reservations about whether she could live up to such lofty standards—and whether he saw her clearly.

His fingers continued to caress her face. "Is it any wonder that I panicked when I learned you had accepted Wickham's offer?"

No man could have conjured that speech on the spot. "Um…I…did not know," she stuttered out the words.

"I hid it from you and from myself," he murmured, bending his head toward hers. His intention was clear, and Elizabeth made no effort to pull away. Her feet were rooted to the path. This kiss was sweet, without the raging passion of the previous day. It started with a mere brushing of their lips and grew steadily more insistent until they both needed to catch their breath.

When they finally pulled apart, she nervously surveyed the surrounding area. Fortunately, that part of the park was sparsely populated, but still… "Mr. Darcy, we are in public."

He smiled gently at her, apparently unconcerned. "Perhaps I can remedy that difficulty." Taking her hand, he led her to a copse of fir trees. He pushed through the branches and guided her into a small empty space in the middle. They were mostly shielded from prying eyes but still within the confines of the park.

Elizabeth shivered. What did he intend to do?

Her reaction caught his attention; he regarded her solemnly. "Elizabeth, if I do anything you dislike, tell me immediately, I pray you." He waited until she had nodded. "I do not wish to make you uncomfortable."

The next kiss contained all the passion the previous one had lacked. He kissed her as if she supplied the air he needed to survive. Each stroke of his tongue, each caress of his lips, told her how desperately he wanted her to believe in his passion for her. It was overwhelming, an assault on her senses she had not anticipated. Mr. Darcy's arms held her tightly against his body as if he could never let her go.

As they parted, her head was spinning, and she needed to grip his arm to maintain her balance. After a moment, Mr. Darcy released her and stepped backward. "Forgive me, Miss Bennet."

Her eyebrows knit together. For what was he apologizing? All she could think was that she hoped he would do it again.

He stared at the ground, cheeks red. "I wished you to believe the sincerity of my words, and instead I assault you as I did yesterday."

Elizabeth swallowed hard. It was difficult to admit to her own wantonness, but she would not allow him to labor under a delusion. "Sir, had I found the kiss less than desirable, you would know it."

As he smiled, his fingers touched his swollen lip gingerly. "I suppose I would." She would not apologize for striking him yesterday; he deserved it. "May I hope, then, that you found my kisses acceptable?"

She shivered; something in his humble, almost plaintive, tone touched her deeply. But still she was not at all prepared to give her unqualified approval. She did not want to give him the impression that she was prepared to accept his offer. "Yes…they were quite…pleasant." It was a ridiculously inadequate word to describe the effect they had had on her, but he gave her a slow smile, seemingly encouraged by the vague compliment.

A drop of water hit her sleeve. When Elizabeth glanced up, another drop hit her cheek. "Oh no! It is raining."

"That *is* a shame," Mr. Darcy said with an expression of disappointment. No doubt he had planned for additional kisses. "Will you allow me to accompany you back to Gracechurch Street? I do not want you to get caught in a downpour."

Why did the thought of more time—even ten more minutes—with Mr. Darcy give her such an illicit thrill? Truth be told, the thrill had always been there, but only now did she allow herself to acknowledge and indulge it. "Yes, of course. Thank you."

"Might I wait upon you tomorrow and join you for another walk?"

"Yes, and if you are very fortunate, I may even tell you what time I plan to venture out, so you need not lurk on my uncle's doorstep."

He laughed.

The downpour held off as they hurried back to Gracechurch Street. They spoke of inconsequential topics, but Elizabeth was struck by how unexpectedly pleasant she had found the entire walk to be. The taste of his kisses lingered on her lips. She should not have allowed such liberties, but he was proving difficult to resist. Now that she knew of his interest in her—and his *love*—it was doubly hard to resist the urge to touch and be touched.

She was well aware that he had offered her marriage, and she had not yet responded. Earlier in the day she had been tempted to throw the offer back in his face no matter the consequences, but now she was pleased she had not announced an irrevocable decision. She was grateful he had not pressed her for an answer today; she was vacillating more than ever before. She had received his words and his kisses with great pleasure but knew she should not make the mistake of deciding her entire future based on a pleasant walk.

If there were a chance she might accept Mr. Darcy, then perhaps she should give her aunt and uncle an opportunity to know him better. Improved acquaintance might soften their opinion of him, and they might give her the benefit of their advice.

They arrived at the Gardiners' house, huddled under a little portico outside the door. This was the point at which he should bid her adieu, but he had made no move to disengage her arm from his and peered down at her with something resembling tenderness.

She swallowed hard. "M-Mr. Darcy, would you perhaps like to come in for a while and enjoy a cup of tea before you must venture out in the rain once more?"

He froze for a moment, evidently surprised by the invitation. "Certainly. I thank you."

They were greeted by Shaw, whose eyes widened slightly at the sight of Mr. Darcy in Elizabeth's company, but she took their outer garments without comment. Elizabeth led the way to the drawing room, surprised to hear more than one male voice. Her aunt and uncle must have visitors. Only right before she opened the drawing room door did she recognize the second, unexpected male voice, but by then it was too late; she had already turned the knob.

She pushed the door open to reveal the Gardiners conversing with their guest. "Hello, Lizzy," said her uncle. "Your father has just arrived."

Chapter Ten

Elizabeth's expression suggested that she had not expected to see her father in the Gardiners' drawing room. Darcy was scarcely less surprised. Mr. Gardiner must have sent Mr. Bennet an express immediately after the events of the previous day for him to have arrived so speedily.

"Papa!" Elizabeth hesitated on the threshold for a moment, throwing a strained look over her shoulder at Darcy, but there was no escaping their fate. Then she rushed forward to embrace her father.

As she vacated the doorway, Darcy became visible to the room's occupants. Mr. Gardiner started, glaring at Darcy with his fists clenched. Mrs. Gardiner gave him a cold look full of contempt. When Elizabeth's father released his daughter, he viewed Darcy with the enthusiasm one would greet an unexpected rash. His expression suggested that, had he been younger, he might have challenged Darcy to a duel.

Darcy could hardly blame them. He would feel the same in their place should he be confronted with a man who had treated Georgiana in such an infamous manner. He had made a grievous error in judgment and was supremely fortunate that Elizabeth seemed inclined to forgive him.

Elizabeth seated herself on the sofa beside her father, but Darcy remained hovering in the doorway, unsure if he would be invited to sit. However, invited or not, he owed everyone an apology. Darcy took a deep breath. "Mr. Bennet, I must beg your pardon for the insult I offered to your daughter."

The other man raised an eyebrow. "Why beg my forgiveness, Mr. Darcy? Apparently, you have Lizzy's."

Elizabeth colored. "Papa—"

Darcy wanted to snap at the man for causing his daughter such mortification and reminded himself that his own actions were responsible for the current situation.

This could take some time; Darcy seated himself without waiting for an invitation. "Miss Bennet has been quite generous in forgiving my misjudgment," Darcy said through gritted teeth. "I feel very fortunate to have made progress in securing any measure of her good opinion."

"Misjudgment?" Bennet growled. "That is a pretty word to describe laying your hands on her person."

Darcy narrowed his focus to Elizabeth's father, stifling the impulse to bark out an angry retort. Digging his nails into the palms of his hands, he chose his words carefully. "I have made what amends I can. I have made her the offer of my hand."

Bennet leveled a gaze at him. "Forgive me if I do not believe your word is worth much."

Gardiner gasped. It was quite an insult, but Darcy managed to conceal his flinch. The man was justified in his anger. Bennet continued, his voice trembling, "I understood you gave your word to your cousin to marry *her*."

How had that rumor reached Hertfordshire? "I have no understanding or engagement with my cousin. My aunt wishes such an alliance and speaks of it as a settled matter, but neither Anne nor I wish to marry." He allowed his disdain for the idea to show on his face.

Bennet was holding himself very still, one hand clutching the arm of the sofa. "So I am to believe that you would actually marry Elizabeth?"

Darcy took a deep breath through his nose; he always struggled to control his temper when his honor was impugned. "I have said that I would." He flashed a glance at Elizabeth's stony face. "If she will have me."

Bennet stiffened. "You have not accepted his hand?" he said to his daughter.

"No," she responded. Darcy had to admire her sangfroid. In the face of her father's disdain, most other women would have felt the need to justify such a decision and pleaded their right to delay an answer. But if she had been any other woman, Darcy would not have wanted her with an almost physical ache.

Bennet's countenance showed no surprise at her response; he must know his daughter well. However, he continued to glare at her. Many fathers would blame their daughters for what had occurred in the garden, although the wrongdoing had been on Darcy's part. It was the way of the world to blame the woman in such situations. Hopefully Bennet was not of that ilk. Unease prickled along Darcy's spine. What if her father berated and belittled her? How could Darcy protect her from her own father?

"She must marry him," Gardiner said to Bennet. "Surely you see that."

Bennet gave his brother a venomous look. "I do *not* see that. I would prefer to risk scandal than have my daughter marry this blackguard."

Darcy's hands clenched at the insult, although he admired Bennet's insistence on ensuring his daughter's happiness. Bennet directed his glare at Darcy. "You have proven how unworthy you are of Lizzy. Fortunately, she has shown superior judgment in refusing to bow to your attempts to force the matter." He stood, addressing the room at large. "Well, this may be easily arranged. I shall pay off the servants and take Lizzy home to Hertfordshire with me. Then we may forget the whole, sorry business." He pointed an accusatory finger at Darcy. "And you, sir, will never come near Longbourn or Lizzy again."

A fist squeezed Darcy's heart, making it hard to breathe. His encounter with Elizabeth in the park had helped to lift some of his black despair, but now her father threatened to separate them forever. Darcy's eyes flickered to Elizabeth, who was frowning at her father. Was it because she did not believe his plan was feasible or because she did not wish to leave London—and Darcy? How he longed for it to be the latter, but her expression revealed nothing.

The Gardiners both stood as well; their nervous, jerky movements betrayed doubts that the matter was as easily solved as Bennet believed.

Darcy remained seated. "There is the matter of Wickham," he drawled.

The Gardiners immediately sat, but Bennet slowly turned his head to Darcy, fixing him with a baleful stare. "Ah yes, Wickham. The man to whom Lizzy would be engaged if not for your interference."

"That would be a grave mistake," Darcy said, struggling to keep his voice level. "I would do anything to prevent Eliz—Miss Bennet from an alliance with Wickham. He cannot be trusted."

Bennet's eyes narrowed further, and he folded his arms over his chest. "And why is that?"

Darcy was not about to reveal Georgiana's shame to a group of near strangers. "The matter is private, although Miss Bennet knows the story."

Bennet snorted. "So we are to take your word that the man is a reprobate, although the evidence suggests *you* are the one who cannot be trusted?" Darcy flinched at the accusation.

"I believe his story; Mr. Wickham is not to be trusted," Elizabeth said quietly.

All eyes turned to her. "What lies has he been telling you, Lizzy?" her father asked.

She lifted her chin. "I know the story, and I find it credible, but I am not at liberty to discuss the particulars."

The back of Darcy's neck was moist with sweat. The Gardiners knew Georgiana had visited Elizabeth; would they make the connection that she was the one who had changed Elizabeth's mind about Wickham? Would they guess why? He had not foreseen that consequence of allowing Georgiana to visit Gracechurch Street.

Bennet threw his hands up in the air in exasperation. "So I simply must accept your word for it?"

"Do you have any reason to believe my word is suspect, sir?" Elizabeth asked with an arched brow. Only at that moment did Darcy realize she was trembling in anger.

Bennet sat, mopping his brow with a handkerchief. "He has turned your head somehow, Lizzy. Is it his fortune? I would not see you wed to a man you could not respect—no matter how many carriages he can buy you."

Elizabeth shot to her feet. "I did not realize you held such a low opinion of my judgment!"

Father and daughter glared at each other for a moment. "Are you saying you wish to marry the man who has treated you so abominably?" Bennet asked, standing to look his daughter in the eye.

"I am saying," she said slowly and precisely, "that I would like to know Mr. Darcy better to ascertain whether I would like to accept the offer of his hand."

She is magnificent. Despite his anxiety over the situation, Darcy could not prevent a swell of pride.

Bennet was as still as a statue for a moment. Then he reared back. "Absolutely not! Have you forgotten that we all know he is a difficult, unpleasant sort of man with the devil's own pride? I will not give my daughter to such a man."

"But—"

"Not under any circumstances! And certainly not under these!" he thundered.

Elizabeth's face had grown quite pale, and Darcy studied it carefully for future reference. This was how she appeared when she was hot with anger. "I am not *yours* to give," she said through clenched teeth. "I am my own."

Bennet blinked. He struck Darcy as the kind of father who rarely exerted his authority in the family. Apparently, he had not expected such defiance from his daughter. More the fool he.

He grabbed Elizabeth by the upper arm, tugging her toward the door. "We may discuss your authority on the way home to Longbourn."

She pulled her arm from his grasp and backed away, wide-eyed like a cornered animal. Darcy realized he was on his feet, apparently ready to defend her even from her own father.

"I do not wish to return to Hertfordshire as of yet," she said.

"I will not permit you to remain here," Bennet said in a low voice. "Your uncle will not keep you if I say no."

Elizabeth started, her eyes darting from her father to her uncle. But then she muttered, "Very well."

Darcy's heart sank. Given time he might be able to win her affection, but once she was at Longbourn, her family could forbid her to see him.

Her father nodded approvingly. "I am pleased you have seen rea—"

"I am not finished," Elizabeth spoke over him. "If I may not stay at Gracechurch Street, I will remove myself to Darcy House to visit my friend Miss Darcy."

Stunned silence followed this pronouncement.

Elizabeth turned her fierce stare on Darcy. "If I am welcome, Mr. Darcy?"

Inwardly, Darcy was dancing with joy at the prospect, although the anger in her face was a bit alarming.

"Of course," he responded immediately, thinking through the ramifications. Would Mrs. Annesley be a sufficient chaperone for both Elizabeth and Georgiana? Should he ask his aunt to visit as well?

"I assume you have secured a special license?" she asked.

This is unexpected. Darcy's heart beat faster. "Y-Yes, I have," he stammered. Events were proceeding at an alarming speed, and it was somewhat disconcerting not to be the one putting them in motion. But he had no interest in objecting; he would get what he wanted.

"We could be married tomorrow," she said in flat voice, looking at her father.

Darcy's eyes widened. Perhaps he would not need Mrs. Annesley after all. "Indeed," he responded, trying to not to smile.

Bennet regarded Darcy with narrowed eyes. "You would actually marry her tomorrow?"

Darcy was getting tired of answering this question. "I have a special license, and the priest at the parish church is available to perform the ceremony." He folded his arms over his chest, boldly returning the other man's gaze. He did not like the way Bennet had questioned his honor, but even worse, he had upset Elizabeth.

Bennet's eyes traveled back to his daughter, who stared at her father, tightlipped and defiant. For a long moment nobody said anything. Finally, Bennet threw his arms in the air. "Very well. If you wish to remain at Gracechurch Street, then remain!" he growled, throwing himself back on the sofa. "But I shall remain as well."

Elizabeth's shoulders relaxed. "Thank you, Papa. I would prefer to have some time to consider Mr. Darcy's offer."

Darcy quelled a pang of disappointment, telling himself it would be worth the wait if they could marry with her family's approval.

Now that much of the tension had leaked from the room, Bennet eyed Darcy with half a smile. "Are you certain you want her, Darcy? You see what a troublesome creature she can be."

Darcy's eyes remained fixed on Elizabeth's face as he responded. "Indeed, I am quite certain. I long for nothing more in the world."

She smiled at him, and his heart stopped.

***

Mr. Darcy had departed. Dinner had been eaten, and the evening port had been consumed. Elizabeth's aunt and uncle had just bid everyone good night. Elizabeth was alone with her father for the first time that day.

He had been reading the newspaper, but now he was just staring into the dwindling flames of the fireplace. The silence was thick and uncomfortable.

"Are you very angry with me, Papa?" she asked.

His head shook slowly. "Mostly I am angry with myself for pushing you into such defiance." He chuckled. "I should have known better. You never take the easy path."

She gave him a wan smile. "I suppose not."

"When I received your uncle's letter, my only thought was to come to London and rescue from that dreadful man." He rubbed his face with a weary hand. "It did not occur to me that you did not wish to be rescued."

He did not intend his words as a barb, but Elizabeth winced nonetheless. She rose from the settee and seated herself on the ottoman opposite her father's chair. The fire gently warmed one side of her body while the other grew cooler.

Her father spoke before she had a chance to gather her thoughts. "I did not realize you held Mr. Darcy in such high esteem."

Elizabeth blinked. It was true that her opinion of the man had changed considerably in only a day. The last twenty-four hours had been a wild ride. "I did not initially, but I have since learned that much of what we know of him is a lie."

"But what of his cruelty toward Mr. Wickham?"

Elizabeth stared at the fire, choosing her words carefully. "I spoke with Miss Darcy. While I am not at liberty to disclose the substance of that conversation, suffice it to say, she made it clear that Mr. Wickham is by no means a respectable man. I am quite happy I dissolved our engagement."

"And you trust the story?"

Elizabeth thought of Miss Darcy's trembling hands and broken voice as she told her tale. "I do."

Her father leaned forward, taking both her hands in his. "If you were deceived by Mr. Wickham, then I was as well."

Elizabeth bowed her head. "It was horrifying to learn how wrong I had been."

"It must have been quite a blow." Her father stroked her hair gently.

"My judgment has been quite flawed." Her stomach did a sickly lurch as she recalled exactly how flawed. "That is why I ask you to give Mr. Darcy a second chance."

"Do you plan to accept his offer, then?" he asked, his brow creased with concern. Somehow the past day had aged her father.

Elizabeth bit her lip, worrying a ring on her finger. "I plan to make no decision immediately. I believe I was overly hasty in accepting Mr. Wickham." And she had nearly ruined her future. Elizabeth could not help but be grateful to Mr. Darcy for preventing such a disaster.

"I intend to take the time to become familiar with Mr. Darcy. However, my opinion of him has improved upon further acquaintance." Her eyes met her father's. "The same may happen with you."

He squeezed her hands. "Perhaps. I will try to become further acquainted with him."

"Thank you, Papa."

***

Caroline Bingley sniffed disdainfully at the bench before removing a handkerchief from her reticule, wiping the offending object, and gingerly taking a seat. Her gown was most expensive; she would be quite vexed if it was soiled.

She was not particularly fond of the out of doors, but if she must be exposed to the elements at this time of year, she should at least be in Hyde Park where the company was congenial. Unfortunately, today's rendezvous could not be witnessed by anyone she knew, so she was forced to wait on this miserable scrap of land near the river.

And, naturally, Mr. Wickham was late again. She fumed in silence for several minutes, watching every passerby eagerly in hopes of seeing his face. Finally, he strolled into view, his hands stuffed insouciantly in his pockets.

Caroline bit back the impulse to snap at him; he was not a servant to be ordered around. But she wished she could voice her opinion of his rumpled clothes and overly long hair. He was reputed to be charming with women, but Caroline did not find him at all attractive.

Mr. Wickham settled next to her and draped one arm over the back of the bench. She stiffened at this familiarity but said nothing. Unfortunately, she needed this odious man's cooperation.

"Well?" she asked when he did not seem inclined to speak. "Did you take care of it? Are you betrothed to Eliza Bennet?"

Mr. Wickham's expression was not particularly triumphant; a knot of anxiety began to form in Caroline's stomach. "I encountered some difficulties," he said slowly.

"Of what kind?" she snapped.

"Of the Darcy kind."

"Did she agree to marry you?"

"Yes, but—"

"Good!" She clapped her hands together.

"But," Wickham's voice rose, "Darcy arrived right after, and…well…he kissed her."

"Kissed her!" Caroline's hand flew to her throat. How disgusting. The words conjured up such horrible images.

Wickham scratched the back of his head. "He made a big show of it. I believe he was attempting to compromise her so she could not marry me."

Caroline's nostrils flared. "Nonsense! He would not do such a thing. Not to her. He was simply drawn in—momentarily—by her arts and allurements."

Wickham's shrug eloquently conveyed: "If you say so."

"He could not possibly have any lasting attachment to her," Caroline muttered. "She is so…skinny, and her skin is so brown."

Wickham raked Caroline with a dubious—and, to her mind, insolent—stare from head to toe. "She is pretty enough."

She wanted to throw things. She was paying the blackguard! Could he not at least assure her that she was prettier?

Wickham shifted on the bench. "Then yesterday I received a note from Miss Bennet saying she could not marry me after all."

Caroline nearly fell off the bench. "Good heavens! Are they betrothed?" That would be a disaster.

"I doubt it. She seemed very angry when he just up and kissed her. She punched him pretty hard."

How unladylike! Still… Caroline settled back into the bench. "Good, good."

"Of course, ten thousand a year is quite an inducement…"

Good Lord, why must the man remind her? "I know." She could not fathom what Mr. Darcy saw in the upstart country miss, and Eliza Bennet's behavior was even more inexplicable. While Caroline would not have preferred to be kissed in a public place, she would not have objected too strenuously if Mr. Darcy were doing the kissing. She certainly would not strike him; that was unforgiveable.

Wickham stared glumly at the river. "I think the whole business is hopeless. Although I am not returning your money," he added hastily.

"Nonsense!" Caroline exclaimed. "We must simply find another way to separate them."

"What can we do?"

"Can you regain her trust?"

Wickham considered for a long moment. "Possibly…I doubt Darcy will have told her everything about me."

Caroline had no doubt Wickham had behaved detestably toward Mr. Darcy, but the details were irrelevant. This wretch was the only person at the moment who could prevent the master of Pemberley from marrying the wrong woman.

"I doubt I could get her to agree to another engagement," Wickham volunteered.

She waved her hand. "That is immaterial. You must simply separate her from Mr. Darcy by whatever means possible. Lie to her. Seduce her. Tell her what she needs to hear. Whatever it takes."

Wickham stroked his chin dubiously. "But what if she refuses to listen to me?"

Caroline shrugged. "Then compromise her."

"Darcy already compromised her!"

She rolled her eyes. "Then do so again!"

Wickham frowned as if doing a complicated mathematics problem. "Can a woman be compromised twice?"

She hated relying on such an idiot. "Of course, she can! Just compromise her...*more thoroughly*. Even you can do that."

Wickham looked a little sick. "Y-Yes. But Darcy will not like it."

"It will be too late for Mr. Darcy to do anything by that point," Caroline said. "He will lose interest."

"This is quite a bit more effort on my part," Wickham said, scanning the area for observers. "You did promise me more money."

Caroline gritted her teeth. "I promised you more money when you accomplished our objective, which you have singularly failed to do."

Wickham crossed his arms and settled back into the bench. "I am risking getting punched by Darcy or arrested—or both—while you lounge in luxury giving orders."

Caroline sighed. She had been prepared for this objection but had hoped to obtain his assistance without additional payment. She reached into her reticule and extracted a small pouch of coins. "For your pains"— she dropped them into Wickham's outstretched hand—"but I shall give you no more until Elizabeth Bennet is gone from Mr. Darcy's life. Then he will surely propose to me."

Wickham opened the pouch and stared greedily at the coins. "Consider it done."

Chapter Eleven

The morning after her father arrived, Elizabeth was surprised by another visit from Mr. Darcy. Considering how abominably he had been abused by her father, Elizabeth had rather expected he would stay at home and avoid the entire Bennet clan. But he was sober and even-tempered and greeted her father cordially. He then extended an invitation for the entire Gardiner family as well as Elizabeth and her father to join him and his sister in a box for a performance at Astley's Amphitheatre.

He could not have chosen a better invitation. Although the Gardiners had attended Astley's before, they were happy to have an activity which included their children and eager to see the Amphitheatre's special performance for the Christmas season. Elizabeth's father, who disliked London, had grumbled that he might as well go while he was in town, but she could see that he was curious about the famous show.

Elizabeth had never attended a show at Astley's and was looking forward to it with eager anticipation as they all climbed into Mr. Darcy's carriage. Unfortunately, he was not aboard as the space was crowded enough with four adults and numerous young Gardiners sitting on everyone's laps. The barouche was well-sprung and quite comfortable without being ostentatious. Her father noted all the details; Elizabeth could see that he was impressed despite himself.

Mr. Darcy was waiting to hand her out of the carriage when it rolled to a stop in front of the theatre. "Miss Bennet." Touching his hand was like touching a burning ember. She was shocked at the electricity that traveled up her arm and spread throughout her body from a simple contact between their fingers. The slight widening of Mr. Darcy's eyes suggested that he was as affected as she was. If only she could step closer to him and explore what was happening between them. If she could understand what occurred behind that stern demeanor. Was he feeling the same way she was?

In truth, she did not believe anyone in her life had ever regarded her quite the way he did. His dark eyes beheld her with a warmth she would not have believed was within his capabilities. But there was also a hint of apprehension in his expression, as if all his hopes and dreams rested upon her shoulders. It gave her a heady sense of power over such a formidable, self-contained man. Yet her nerves also buzzed with anxiety as his expectations weighed her down. What if she decided she did not wish to be married to him?

Her father cleared his throat, and Elizabeth realized she had been clasping Mr. Darcy's hand longer than was proper. Coloring, she took a step back from him. He tore his eyes from hers and greeted the Gardiners and her father.

"Please allow me to introduce my sister, Miss Georgiana Darcy, and my cousin, Colonel Richard Fitzwilliam." Only then did Elizabeth notice two people standing behind Mr. Darcy. Miss Darcy was as pretty as Elizabeth remembered, but she was plainly shy in so much company and would not look directly at anyone in the party. The colonel was a plain man with an open, unassuming countenance. He greeted everyone with easy, friendly manners even as he regarded Elizabeth with undisguised curiosity.

Before leading the way through the crowds, Mr. Darcy offered Elizabeth his arm while his cousin took Miss Darcy's. She felt quite important on the arm of such an elegantly dressed man and at the front of such a procession. Heads turned their way, and women whispered behind their fans as they proceeded through the crowds. What would it be like to have this experience everywhere she went? Elizabeth could not quite imagine it.

Their box was large, elegantly appointed, and quite close to the stage. Mr. Darcy seated Elizabeth at the front and took the seat beside hers. Behind them, her father cleared his throat as if to object to the arrangement, but Mr. Darcy fixed him with a steady gaze and he subsided. The others settled into chairs arranged throughout the rest of the box, although everyone would get a good view of the performance.

Some of the younger Gardiners crowded up to the edge of the box, peering down at the stage and the throngs of people in amazement. Elizabeth was surprised when Miss Darcy knelt down next to young Harry and little Cassandra, chatting with them about what they would see. Soon she was surrounded by the entire crowd of Gardiner children. Apparently, Miss Darcy's shyness did not extend to children.

The Amphitheatre itself was different from any theatre Elizabeth had ever seen. There was the customary proscenium stage, but in front of it, a large ring, sprinkled with sawdust, had been laid on the floor. Since Astley's was primarily a riding exhibition, Elizabeth guessed the ring was where the horses would run. Ingenious ramps led between the ring and the stage.

She did not know whether the nervous flutters in her stomach resulted more from the anticipation of seeing the famous show or mingled excitement and anxiety over Mr. Darcy's proximity. Every time she glanced in his direction, she found his dark eyes upon her, sending excited thrills down her spine.

Then the performance began, immediately exceeding all of Elizabeth's expectations. Horses and riders thundered across the stage, down the ramps, around the ring, and onto the stage again, moving so swiftly that their colorful costumes were a blur. It was a dazzling exhibition.

During the acts that followed, Elizabeth could not decide which was more thrilling: the rope twirler or the juggler or the man who rode two horses at once. Then there was a rider who rode three horses at once!

She could not stop applauding the trick riders who jumped on and off horseback with ease, grabbing swords from the floor without even breaking stride. Next there was a man who juggled while on horseback. The horses were bedecked with garlands of greenery and red velvet ribbons. A group of mummers performed a short Christmas play. Elizabeth felt fortunate she could see the performance at Christmastide.

In between these acts, the clowns kept the crowd laughing. Elizabeth particularly liked the male clown who chased after a female clown with a piece of mistletoe, trying to steal a kiss. Even her father was chuckling.

A few minutes into the performance, Mr. Darcy's hand reached over and enclosed hers. He regarded her anxiously—perhaps concerned that she would pull away—but relaxed when she smiled at him. The touch of his hand should have been odd, but instead it was warm and comforting.

She was almost sorry when the interval arrived, breaking the performance's magical spell. Elizabeth had no need to leave the box, but the Gardiners took her father to meet some acquaintances they had noticed in the audience, while the colonel and Miss Darcy herded the children out in search of refreshments and an opportunity to run about. Suddenly, Elizabeth was alone with Mr. Darcy.

She stood, seeking a better view of the theatre. "It is wonderful! Thank you, Mr. Darcy, for inviting us."

"Please call me William," his deep voice rumbled.

"But—" Elizabeth was about to object to such impropriety. Then she reminded herself that the man had proposed to her. She swallowed. "I will...try."

This earned a small smile. "I cannot tell you how much it pleases me to see you so enjoying yourself."

Oh, Lord, he was so close and so distracting. She needed to find something to talk about—something to think about besides his lopsided smile. She said the first thing that came into her head. "I wish Jane were here. She loves riding, and her spirits could do with some improvement."

His brows drew together. "She is out of spirits?"

Oh. Elizabeth had not meant to divulge that. "Well…since she hurt her ankle…" Mr. Darcy—William—nodded. An impulse Elizabeth did not understand insisted that she be honest with this man. "But really the melancholy started when your party left Netherfield."

William stiffened. There was something in his eyes…Could he verify Elizabeth's suspicions about why they had left Hertfordshire? Had Mr. Bingley's sisters insisted he give up Jane? She gazed down at the audience, attempting a casualness she did not feel. "It was a hard blow for her when Mr. Bingley departed. Do you know when he will return?"

His eyes widened, giving him a slightly panicked appearance. "No, I do not." The words emerged in a rush. "He has not confided his plans to me."

Elizabeth nodded, trying not to think about Jane's wan face upon their parting.

William shifted uneasily and turned his eyes toward the stage. The movement tugged at her hand, and Elizabeth realized their fingers were still entangled. Heavens! Had anyone noticed? A quick glance at the audience confirmed that nobody appeared to be watching them, but if they should…

The sensible act would be to release his hand, but Elizabeth knew by now that she was unlikely to do the sensible thing when it came to Mr. Darcy—so, of course, she wanted to continue holding his hand. She pulled him toward the back of the box, where the shadows and the folds of the curtain would shield them from view.

Mr. Darcy—William—raised his eyebrows in surprise but did not object. She shrugged self-consciously. "One is so exposed in a box. I desire more privacy."

William did not respond but immediately took advantage of the dim lighting to cup her cheek with his hand. "I am in agony, Elizabeth," he groaned. "Can you give me any hope that you will accept my suit, or is this all in vain?"

Did he indeed believe his situation could possibly be as hopeless as all that? Did he not note the signs that her opinion of him was improving, softening? She swallowed, finding it difficult to meet eyes so full of desperation. "Indeed, sir, I would not hold the hand of a man I had firmly decided against. I am not prepared to give you an answer, but there is reason for hope. Ample reason."

His forehead creased. "But your father's objections…"

"He and I spoke last night. He is not as intransigent as he appeared at first, but rather he is willing to reserve judgment."

William's head was bowed. "That is good to hear."

Elizabeth could restrain herself no longer. The memory of the kisses in the garden and the park haunted her. She could feel the ghostly presence of his lips on hers—and she wanted more. More contact with this man. More touching. Stepping forward, she reached out a hand to touch his arm, his shoulder.

"Oh, Good Lord, Elizabeth," William moaned as his other hand wound around her waist and pulled her gently toward him. His lips met hers for a soft kiss. As he deepened the kiss, one hand moved to the back of her head while the other pulled her more tightly against him. They moved in harmony, as if their entire bodies participated in the kiss. His tongue licked along the seam of her lips. She parted them almost involuntarily, and suddenly his tongue was in her mouth!

***

Darcy could not believe Elizabeth was allowing him such liberties. In the dark recesses of his mind, he knew he should not be taking advantage of her momentary pliancy, but such self-control was far beyond his capacity at the moment. Touching her…feeling her warmth against his…it was so exhilarating that he could not help discovering new places on her body to explore. The more of her he touched, the more he wanted to touch.

One hand had traveled up her back and was daringly caressing the bare skin of her shoulder blades. He waited for her to stiffen and pull away, but instead she moaned and snuggled closer in his arms. He was lost.

Their tongues entangled, dueled, and created amazing sensations. Simultaneously, his fingers inched under the edge of her bodice in the back. Forbidden territory, but the skin was so soft. So tempting. His fingertips traced down her spine, vertebra by vertebra, deeper and deeper under the back of her dress. She arched her back and moaned, the sound further enflaming his desire.

He pressed her against the wall, the better to feel the soft pillows of her breasts and the roundness of her stomach. The yielding softness of her body and the hardness of his. They were so close he could feel the rapid beat of her heart.

Now his other hand was creeping under the edge of the neckline in the front of her gown. What would her breasts feel like in his hands? At the last minute, Darcy ripped his mouth from hers. "Good Lord, Elizabeth, tell me to stop!"

Elizabeth stared up at him, blinking owlishly.

"I must stop now while I may still call myself a gentleman," he panted, turning his head down and away, unable to meet her eyes lest his desire combust again. He had expected her to stop him, to pull away or slap him or object. What did it mean that she had done none of those things?

When he had finally mastered himself sufficiently, he dared to look back at Elizabeth, expecting to see condemnation. Instead, her eyes held a kind of wildness, almost frustration that he had interrupted their mutual pleasure. A distressed noise emerged from deep in her throat. Was it possible that her desire for him matched his for her? Could he possibly be that fortunate?

Pulling on the front of his waistcoat, she leaned forward for another kiss. Unable to completely resist her touch, Darcy placed both hands on her waist and brushed her lips softly before pulling away with great reluctance. "Not here, my love. Although I will gladly kiss you elsewhere at any time of your choosing."

She was still breathing hard, and her eyes were round with wonder. "H-How...do you cause me to forget myself so?"

Darcy shook his head slowly. "I could ask the same of you."

Her hand stroked the front of his waistcoat, causing him to shiver in reaction. "Is it always so?" she asked. "Kissing?"

He was the only man she had ever kissed like that. How thrilling. "Never," he whispered. "It is *never* like that in my experience."

She smiled slowly and a little bit wickedly. "Mr. Darcy—"

"Elizabeth, *please* call me William," he sighed.

"Very well, William—"

"Mr. Darcy!" thundered Bennet's voice from behind him.

Darcy jumped backward from Elizabeth, nearly stumbling over a chair. No doubt his expression displayed his guilt.

Red-faced, Bennet trembled with rage. "If this is how you conduct yourself, you can hardly call yourself a gentleman, sir!"

Darcy said nothing. Bennet was right. Why could he not prevent himself from touching Elizabeth?

Elizabeth, however, would not tolerate such treatment. With a single step, she inserted herself between Darcy and her father.

"Out of my way, Lizzy!" Bennet demanded.

She held up her hands to prevent her father from reaching Darcy. "Papa, he did nothing I did not want."

"You are too young to know what you want!" Bennet growled.

Oh no. Darcy could have advised the man that those were the wrong words to say to his daughter.

"Oh?" Elizabeth's face was pale, and her hands clenched at her sides. "How old was Mama again when you married her?" Her voice was a vicious whisper.

Bennet stopped advancing toward Darcy and focused his glare on his daughter. "That was entirely different. Your mother and I were engaged."

Elizabeth put her hands on her hips. "Mr. Darcy has made me the offer of his hand. I am the one who is delaying this engagement."

Despite his anxiety, Darcy was pleased to hear that she considered the engagement merely "delayed."

"Perhaps you should reconsider if this is how the man conducts himself!" her father cried. Fortunately, the hubbub from the crowd in the Amphitheatre drowned out his voice, or the dispute would be quite public.

Elizabeth advanced on her father. "And you never stole a kiss from Mama before the wedding?" Bennet gaped at her; Elizabeth smiled. "I thought so." It was extremely entertaining to see Elizabeth argue her father to a standstill.

Scowling, Bennet threw his arms in the air. "Very well. You have made your point, Lizzy," he conceded with a sad shake of his head, sinking into the first available chair. "I will give you some leeway on this. However, a decision must be made soon. Do you understand?"

Elizabeth tilted her head to the side, coolly considering her father. "Yes, Papa. I will give my decision to Mr. Darcy within the week."

She would? Darcy swallowed, hoping that the decision would be in his favor.

Elizabeth turned back toward Darcy, her stormy countenance giving no hint how she planned to decide. "Mr. Darcy, it appears the second act is about to commence. Shall we take our seats?"

Chapter Twelve

Darcy wanted nothing so much as to camp on the Gardiners' front step until Elizabeth agreed to marry him. However, the Gardiners and Mr. Bennet were quite firm that such behavior would not be welcome.

Therefore, the day following the visit to Astley's, Darcy cast about for a distraction. In the morning he took his horse out for a vigorous ride on Rotten Row. Then he and Richard visited Bingley, whom his cousin had never met; Darcy was pleased at the opportunity to introduce them.

The visit had been pleasant. Because Richard and Bingley were of similar temperaments, Darcy had expected them to delight in each other's company. It had not happened; Bingley had been quiet and morose, and they had departed rather earlier than he expected. As Darcy walked back to Darcy House with Richard, he tried to puzzle out what had happened. Perhaps it was nothing; his judgment might be impaired by Darcy's own distraction over Elizabeth.

Richard cleared his throat. "I have always heard you describe Mr. Bingley as an exuberant man."

"He is," Darcy said. "Usually."

"He appeared...subdued to me," Richard said.

"Hmm." Darcy considered Bingley's manner since...well, since their return from Netherfield. "I believe he wished to pass Christmastide in Hertfordshire, but his sisters would not agree."

"He did seem eager for news of your acquaintances there."

"Yes." Darcy was not completely satisfied with his own behavior regarding their departure from Netherfield, and the more time he spent in Elizabeth's presence, the more uneasy he grew.

Nor was he pleased with his current conduct toward Bingley. Although his friend knew Darcy had contact with Elizabeth in London, he did not know Darcy was courting her. Bingley could rightfully accuse him of hypocrisy, but Darcy had no idea how to broach the subject. Perhaps Richard could help him sort it out. "Bingley...formed an attachment to a woman there."

Richard's eyebrows shot up. "And she spurned his advances?"

"Not at all. She seemed pleased by his attentions, if not overly so. But Miss Bingley thought the family was not desirable, and I did not believe there was a great attachment on her part, so she and I convinced Bingley to leave Hertfordshire." Darcy now realized that his own eagerness to depart was driven in no small part by his desire to separate himself from Elizabeth. Not for the first time, Darcy considered whether Bingley had not been well-served by his advice.

Darcy continued, "Something that Elizabeth said leads me to believe that perhaps her sister harbored real affection for him."

Richard came to an abrupt halt, forcing Darcy to stop as well. "Bingley was courting *Miss Elizabeth's sister?*"

"Yes."

"It is *her* family you and Miss Bingley considered objectionable?" Richard's voice rose in pitch.

"I expressed my reservations about the Bennets to you."

"Damnation, Darcy! Does Bingley know you are courting Miss Elizabeth?"

"No. I thought it best to keep it quiet until—unless—she accepts my hand." Even as he said it, Darcy knew it was an excuse, and a bad one at that.

He would have continued walking, but Richard would not move. "You convinced him to stop courting Elizabeth's sister because the family was undesirable, and then you make an offer to Miss Elizabeth yourself," Richard said slowly. "I thought you valued your friendship with Bingley."

"I do."

"Then what do you think you are about? Whether or not Miss Elizabeth accepts your hand, you could lose Bingley's friendship forever if he learns what you are hiding from him." Richard shook his head at his cousin's stupidity. "Particularly if he ever learns that Elizabeth's sister harbored real affection for him."

Completely still in the middle of the path, Darcy considered his cousin's words. People bustled around them; the carriages and horses sounded from the road. *My God. How have I been so stupid? I had been thinking I was doing Bingley a kindness—rescuing him from the Bennets— and that he would be grateful. I believed I was being kinder to him than I was to myself. But how would I feel about a friend who separated me from Elizabeth?*

Darcy's stomach churned, and for a moment he feared he would be sick. Some of his horror must have shown on his face, for Richard put a reassuring hand on Darcy's shoulder. "What can I do?" Darcy asked. "Bingley will hate me forever if he finds out." *And Elizabeth... Oh, Good Lord, what if Elizabeth learns the truth?*

Richard shrugged. "I do not know, Cuz. What is done is done. But for your own sake, I hope Bingley never finds out. And while you are at it, you had better discover a way to keep the truth from Miss Elizabeth as well."

I am in trouble…

***

Two days before Christmas, the Gardiner house was in a bit of an uproar. The Gardiners' cook was ill, and it was not at all certain she would be well enough to make Christmas dinner. Shaw could cook—in theory—but Aunt Gardiner confided to Elizabeth that the results were disastrous. At this time of year, no other cooks of worth could be hired for a temporary position. Elizabeth's aunt fretted and considered her options but found no solution.

Elizabeth could not help with the cooking since her mother had made it a point to keep her daughters out of the kitchen, but she offered to help her aunt assemble the boxes she was creating for the servants and the workers in Uncle Gardiner's warehouse. Full of clothing, food, and small gifts, the boxes would be given on the day after Christmas, Boxing Day. Elizabeth and her aunt were in the midst of this task at a little table in the drawing room while Elizabeth's uncle and father sat by the fire discussing politics.

Shaw opened the door. "Mr. Wickham is here, ma'am," she announced to Aunt Gardiner.

Elizabeth's cheerful mood evaporated as all eyes in the room turned to her. She kept her face carefully blank as her aunt told Shaw to show him into the drawing room. Elizabeth had expected Mr. Wickham to avoid Gracechurch Street, but perhaps he believed he had something to gain by convincing everyone of the rightness of his cause.

"Mr. Wickham!" As the younger man, quite handsome in his regimentals, entered the room, Elizabeth's father stood and shook his hand warmly. Aunt and Uncle Gardiner likewise greeted Mr. Wickham with a cordiality that had been notably absent in their interactions with Mr. Darcy. *How unfair. He went to a great deal of trouble to host a lovely evening at Astley's, and yet they still prefer this scoundrel. If only I could tell them Miss Darcy's story!*

Mr. Wickham shot Elizabeth a blinding smile; it *was* hard to resist, she now realized. However, the smile she returned was little more than bared teeth.

Everyone chatted with their guest about the weather and trivialities for a few minutes; Elizabeth said little. Finally, Elizabeth's father asked Mr. Wickham, "What brings you to Gracechurch Street today?"

The younger man seemed taken aback by such bluntness, but a smile swiftly appeared on his face. "I hoped for a private conversation with your daughter."

"I wrote to you to discontinue the engagement," she said coldly.

He made a very credible sad face. "Yes, you did, but I had hoped to convince you to reconsider."

"That is very handsome of you, sir." Her father regarded Elizabeth as he spoke to Wickham. "Mr. Darcy took shameless advantage of her."

Elizabeth managed to choke back a cry of frustration.

Mr. Wickham turned soulful eyes to Elizabeth. "I am sorry I did not protect you from his brutal advances. It was all quite sudden."

Her father crossed his arms over his chest. "We do not lay the blame at *your* feet."

How had her life come to such a pass, where her family would rather see her married to this blackguard than to a man of ten times his worth?

But Mr. Wickham smiled so winningly, and his face reflected such open, unassuming good humor, that for a moment even Elizabeth doubted the veracity of the Darcys' story. What if Mr. Wickham *was* sincerely attached to her? What if Miss Darcy had been wrong?

But no, Elizabeth reminded herself. Miss Darcy's tale coincided in every particular with what Elizabeth herself had observed about the man's character.

Her father stood. "We should allow the young people a chance to speak in private," he said to the Gardiners. Uncle Gardiner nodded in agreement, as did Aunt Gardiner, albeit with a concerned expression.

Good Lord! They would leave her alone with the man? "That is not necessary, Papa," Elizabeth said through gritted teeth.

Her father leaned over and spoke into her ear. "Come, you were engaged to the man, albeit briefly. You at least owe him the courtesy of a conversation."

Everyone in the room clearly wanted her to speak with Mr. Wickham, as though her rejection of him were some misunderstanding that could be easily corrected.

"I am certain they have much to discuss," her father said to the Gardiners as they exited the room.

Elizabeth very much doubted this. There were only so many times she could say, "Leave me alone, and do not come near me again." But perhaps a conversation would allow her to finally banish Mr. Wickham from her life.

The moment the door closed behind the others, Mr. Wickham asked, "Would you do me the honor of taking a walk with me?"

Elizabeth wanted any conversation to be brief and final. "I believe it is a little too chilly for a walk today."

"Then a turn about the garden? It will be most refreshing." He stood and offered her his arm.

Elizabeth sighed. "Very well." The sooner it was over, the better. Elizabeth strolled to the door, pointedly ignoring Mr. Wickham's arm.

They traversed the house in silence, donning coats and hats, before venturing into the back garden. The fresh, cool air lifted Elizabeth's spirits, and she wished she could share it with someone else. The wintertime garden had its own stark beauty with bare tree branches framing the sky. It was not quite as warm as it had been upon their previous visit, but the temperature was tolerable.

Mr. Wickham again proffered his arm, and again Elizabeth ignored it, clasping her hands behind her back as she strolled briskly along the pathway. He hastened to catch up. When it became evident that Elizabeth would not speak, Mr. Wickham broke the silence. "I do not know what Darcy told you about me, but it was certainly a lie. The man is the most convincing teller of falsehoods I have ever met."

Elizabeth stifled a laugh but said nothing in response.

"Will you not tell me what he accused me of so that I might clear my name?" he continued. "I love you, Elizabeth. I do not want to lose you."

Now that Elizabeth had heard an authentic declaration of love, she could discern the falseness in Mr. Wickham's. His words contained none of Mr. Darcy's passion and desperation.

Still, she said nothing.

"Will you at least give me the satisfaction of knowing of what I am accused?" His voice took on a pleading tone. "What has Darcy told you?"

Elizabeth stopped to examine a holly bush, heavy with berries; its branches would be very useful for Christmas decorating. "I do not discuss you much with Mr. Darcy," she said to Mr. Wickham with a negligent air. "We usually prefer pleasanter subjects of conversation."

The insult did not register with the man. "Come, you *must* have discussed me with Darcy!"

Elizabeth shook her head as she resumed walking. "Only a little. On the other hand, *Miss Darcy* was an excellent source of information about you."

Mr. Wickham's face turned a satisfying shade of purple. "M-Miss Darcy is in town?" he stammered. "I thought she was at Pemberley."

"I had a most illuminating conversation with her." Elizabeth tapped her lip thoughtfully. "You had told me she was arrogant and proud, but I found her most amiable and pleasant."

A muscle in the man's jaw twitched. "You cannot trust the words of the sister any more than you can trust those of the brother."

Elizabeth's hands clenched into fists. Miss Darcy was far too sweet to be maligned so casually. "I find it curious how many people lie about you, Mr. Wickham. Such a coincidence."

"They *do* lie. I am telling the truth," he said through gritted teeth.

She shrugged. "Perhaps we shall simply have to agree to disagree on that point, Mr. Wickham." He was a good two feet away, and yet it was too close. Her entire body twitched with nervous energy, eager to flee his presence. "I do not believe I have anything further to say to you. Good day, sir." Turning on her heel, she set a brisk pace for the house.

She listened but heard no scuff of boots on the stone pathway— which is why she was taken by surprise when his hand grabbed her elbow and whirled her around to face him. "Do not walk away from me!" he hissed fiercely. "You agreed to be mine, Elizabeth Bennet! Not his!"

With those words, he pulled her toward him and mashed his lips on top of hers.

Elizabeth struggled, but his hands held her upper arms like iron bands. Kissing him was nothing like kissing Mr. Darcy. His tongue was cool and slimy as it forced her lips open and invaded her mouth. She tried to push him away, but he was too strong, and he was too close for her to kick him effectively.

That leaves me only one choice.

She bit down as hard as she could on his tongue.

Mr. Wickham shrieked and tore himself away from her. Blood dotted his lips. *Good.* "You bit me, you chit! You trollop!"

Elizabeth backed away down the path. There was no hope she could outrun him in her skirts, but perhaps if she also called for help… The garden was so large. Would anyone hear her?

The man advanced on her. "I will make you pay for that!" The words were distorted by his swollen tongue. She gathered her skirts in preparation for running, not wanting to take her eyes off her attacker until the last minute.

One minute he was advancing on her; the next something had pulled him from behind, dragging him off the path. A dark figure punched Mr. Wickham, who flew backward and fell like a sack of potatoes, sprawling in the dirt. Now Elizabeth had an unobstructed view of her defender.

"Mr. Darcy!" she cried.

He watched Mr. Wickham warily. "Elizabeth, *please* call me William."

She could not help laughing.

Apparently satisfied that Mr. Wickham would not move, William lifted his eyes to hers and smiled. Stepping over Mr. Wickham's prostrate form, he scanned Elizabeth from head to toe for injury. "Are you well?" In two strides, he had enclosed her in his arms.

"Y-Yes," she sobbed into his waistcoat. "I am p-perfectly f-fine."

"I did not arrive too late?" he asked.

"N-No. Your arrival was quite timely." Peering around his arm, Elizabeth reassured herself that Mr. Wickham was still unconscious.

"Thank God," William murmured, stroking her hair soothingly.

She settled thankfully into his arms, wondering how she could have ever doubted the man. *Why have I not accepted his proposal?* Delay felt ridiculous to her at this point. She peered up at him, refusing to release her grip on his waistcoat. "I should just tell—"

"No." He put a finger to her lips. "Now is not the time or place for such a discussion."

"I suppose an unconscious attacker is not conducive to a romantic atmosphere," she conceded.

William laughed.

"Mr. Darcy!" her father barked. "Release my daughter at once."

"Not again," William muttered. Elizabeth rolled her eyes. Turning her head, she could see both Gardiners as well as her father marching toward them from the house.

"Release her this minute!" her father demanded, stopping a few feet from them.

"No," William replied calmly.

"I beg your pardon?" Her father's mouth fell open.

"Elizabeth is recovering from a shocking experience," William explained. "The man you believed she should wed attacked her and imposed an unwanted kiss upon her."

The newcomers looked past William, gaping at Mr. Wickham lying unconscious in the dirt. "Is this true, Lizzy?" her uncle asked.

Elizabeth nodded, pulling away from William, although she did not release him completely. "He might have hurt me if Mr. Darcy had not arrived when he did."

Her father stared at Mr. Wickham and then at William. "I owe you an apology, Mr. Darcy."

William shook the hand her father offered. "Thank you, sir."

Her father regarded William seriously. Perhaps he was not yet ready to give his blessing for their engagement, but he was closer.

"Perhaps Miss Bennet could use a cup of tea?" William suggested. Elizabeth smiled gratefully at him.

Everything was quickly arranged. Beckett was set to the task of rousing Mr. Wickham and throwing him out on the street. As they strolled back toward the house—Elizabeth on William's arm—Uncle Gardiner asked how William had happened to be in their garden.

"I had arrived for a visit, and Shaw showed me to the drawing room, which was empty," William explained. "As you know, it has a rather nice view of the back garden—and I could see Elizabeth with Wickham. I did not know he would try to kiss her, but I did know she should not be alone with him."

Her father had the grace to look guilty.

William continued, "By the time I arrived out here, she was struggling with him, and…well, I struck him."

"Were you calling to visit Lizzy?" Aunt Gardiner inquired, still white-faced over the events of the day.

"Yes, and to extend an invitation," William said. "Georgiana and I were hoping you would all join us for festivities and dinner on Christmas Day."

Elizabeth's eyes lit up at this exciting prospect, but she said nothing; it was not for her to accept or decline the invitation. Her aunt looked regretful. "I thank you, Mr. Darcy. That is quite a generous offer, but I do not like to leave my children on Christmas."

"I had hoped they would accompany you," William said. "Children make the holidays more festive, and Georgiana would love to see your little ones again."

Aunt Gardiner's expression brightened, and she exchanged looks with her husband, who nodded. "Then it would be our pleasure," she exclaimed.

"Will you be having other guests?" Uncle Gardiner asked.

William shook his head. "Colonel Fitzwilliam will be there, of course, but nobody else. I had originally invited the Bingley family, but Bingley left town on business and is not expected back until after the holiday."

Her uncle nodded, glancing sidelong at her father. "I would be pleased to accept," Mr. Bennet said, "upon one condition." William raised an eyebrow in inquiry. "If you would show me your library. I have heard it is very fine."

William smiled. "It would be my pleasure."

With one hand on William's arm, Elizabeth settled her other hand on her father's arm. "Then it is all settled. We shall celebrate Christmas at Darcy House."

Chapter Thirteen

Naturally, Darcy House was very grand. The front hall soared—two stories in height—and was dominated by a grand staircase clad all in marble. Swags of pine boughs and garlands of ivy and holly decorated the walls and banister. Every candle was lit, making the room glow with warm, yellow light.

Elizabeth was pleased she had worn her most elegant day dress, dark green velvet with white lace trim, but it still felt shabby compared to the grandeur of Darcy House.

The welcome Elizabeth and her family received was anything but shabby, however. Miss Darcy was shy with the adults but overjoyed to see the children again. They danced around her as she distributed sweets. Colonel Fitzwilliam was jovial and welcoming. And Mr. Darcy...

When Elizabeth walked through the door, his eyes lit with a warmth to rival the grandest Yule fire. He said little to her but placed a tender kiss on her cheek, much to her father's consternation.

The visitors were ushered into a very large drawing room, elegantly decorated in blue silk. There was an enormous fire in the hearth, blazing steadily, fueled by what looked like half a tree.

Aunt Gardiner exclaimed, clapping her hands together, "Oh, a true Yule log! So few houses nowadays have a fireplace big enough."

"Did you really keep it going all night?" Elizabeth's young cousin Harry asked.

Mr. Darcy's eyes twinkled as he nodded solemnly to the boy. "Indeed, we did. Georgiana lit it with a piece of last year's log last night, and it blazed strong through the night. We paid one of the kitchen boys a little extra to make sure it did not go out."

Harry's mouth formed a perfect "o" as he watched the fire.

"And we have a real plum pudding, too!" Miss Darcy exclaimed. Several of the children clapped their hands.

One of the maids entered and proceeded to serve wassail to the adults while the children received apple cider.

"And now," William announced, "it is time for the gift giving."

Elizabeth's hand flew to her mouth. "But we have brought nothing for you!" she cried. The Gardiners' tradition was to give presents only to their children on Christmas morning before attending church. Nobody had thought to bring gifts for the adults at Darcy House.

William noticed her expression. "Do not be alarmed. Georgiana and I wanted to give you each something since we are so grateful to have friends here to celebrate Christmas. With the exception of Richard, the rest of our family is in the countryside."

Miss Darcy nodded vigorously. "Your presence is making it so much more festive. And I love to give gifts—especially to children!"

William smiled at his sister. "What Georgiana means is that she loves to shop." She laughed.

Somewhat mollified, Elizabeth took a seat and enjoyed the sight of her young cousins receiving their toys, each carefully wrapped in brown paper. Miss Darcy knew the names and ages of each Gardiner child—an impressive feat considering the size of the brood. The girls received dolls and miniature tea sets while the younger boys were thrilled with lead soldiers. Harry, the oldest, loved his toy sword.

The children were so happy, and the Darcys regarded the fruits of their gift giving with such satisfaction, that Elizabeth had to blink back tears. Although Miss Darcy had obviously been responsible for the purchases, William was equally delighted as he observed the children's reactions to each gift. He would make a good father someday.

Elizabeth had stopped chastising herself for such thoughts. It was pointless.

The gifts continued to flow. Aunt Gardiner received a beautiful silk scarf. Uncle Gardiner crowed over a bottle of French brandy. Elizabeth's father seemed quite pleased with a book of poetry that William had chosen just for him.

Perhaps William had deliberately kept Elizabeth's present for last. He smiled shyly as he handed her a small velvet bag. The size suggested that it was jewelry; perhaps a necklace or ear bobs? Elizabeth's stomach churned. She loved pretty jewelry and had so little, but was it proper to accept a gift from Mr. Darcy? She had given him no answer to his proposal, although at that moment she found herself wondering why in the world she had delayed.

"This is from me and Georgiana," he said solemnly as he placed the little bag on Elizabeth's palm. Clever William. Elizabeth would have fewer reservations about accepting a present from his sister.

She opened the drawstring and upended the bag. A ring tumbled onto her palm. "Oh!" It was designed in an old-fashioned style and contained a single beautiful diamond. A diamond!

"Mr. Darcy," Elizabeth exclaimed, "I cannot possibly accept this! It is far too grand." It must be a family heirloom.

He exchanged a glance and a smile with his sister. "I told you she would object," he said. Then he regarded Elizabeth more solemnly. "It was my mother's, but Georgiana and I both want you to have it. This is the ring my father gave my mother upon their first wedding anniversary."

Elizabeth held it out to Miss Darcy. "Then you should have it."

She shook her head. "I shall wear my mother's wedding ring when I marry. I do not want or need that one."

"It is too much!" Elizabeth exclaimed, although her eyes could not help being drawn to the sparkling diamond. She had never expected to own such a grand piece of jewelry in her life.

Taking her hand in his, Mr. Darcy curled her fingers around the ring in her palm. "No. It is just enough. Even if we do not wed, it is the ring you were born to wear."

Sighing in resignation, Elizabeth slipped the ring on her finger—where it fitted perfectly. It *was* beautiful, but she silently vowed to return it if she and William did not wed.

Tea was served, and everyone enjoyed lemon and chocolate biscuits. Afterward, one of the maids took the children up to the little-used nursery where they could play with their toys or take naps. Miss Darcy watched them leave longingly.

"It is some time until dinner," William said. "What shall we do for amusement?"

"Well, if we were at home…" Elizabeth started.

"Yes?" His eyes were alive with interest.

She exchanged a glance with her father, who had a smile on his face. "We would play charades."

Miss Darcy clapped her hands together. "Can we, William? It has been so long since I played charades!"

The game provided nearly two hours of amusement. Elizabeth would not have expected the proper Mr. Darcy to enjoy the foolishness of such a game, but he threw himself into it with enthusiasm, particularly when he and the colonel competed to see who would win the most points. When the colonel emerged victorious, William was a gracious loser.

Everyone was exhausted from excessive laughter; however, Darcy prevailed upon Georgiana to play some Christmas tunes on the pianoforte. Next Elizabeth played and sang some of her favorites. Mr. Darcy watched her play with a studied intensity one did not usually apply to Christmas music.

The butler entered and announced, "Dinner is served."

Miss Darcy led the way to the dining room, but William held Elizabeth's arm, preventing her from joining the others. "I hope you are enjoying yourself?" he asked.

"Immensely."

"Good. I do not believe I have laughed so much on a Christmas day since…my parents died."

"I must thank you for the gifts, although I believe they are too much."

He shook his head. "You and your family have brought us much more valuable gifts, I assure you."

She smiled and turned toward the dining room, but yet again he held her arm. When she glanced back with a fondly exasperated expression, he pointed upward.

There was mistletoe hanging in the doorway. But… "All of the berries are gone, sir," she observed with a pert smile. "You must await your kiss until next year."

He grinned wickedly and held up his hand, where he was holding a berry between his thumb and forefinger. "I am prepared."

Elizabeth's suspicions were triggered. "Where are the other berries, sir?" she asked with narrowed eyes.

Sheepishly, William dug into his pocket again and produced a handful of berries. "An excuse to kiss you should never be wasted," he said with rakish grin.

She peered at the berries in his hand. "You plan on a great many excuses, do you not?"

"Indeed, so it is best if we begin at once."

Elizabeth rolled her eyes with a smile. "Very well."

She leaned forward, intending to give him a little kiss on the mouth. However, Mr. Darcy had other ideas. Gripping her shoulders, he attacked her mouth with vigor, kissing her with the pent-up need of two days without her. No less eager, Elizabeth clutched the front of his waistcoat, meeting his ardor with her own. When he finally released her, Elizabeth was more than a little dizzy.

"Marry me, Elizabeth," he whispered in her ear, his breath tickling her neck.

It was very tempting to say yes, but what if her reaction to him was mere physical attraction? He was a handsome man—and certainly his wealth was tempting. But what of her heart? Amidst this onslaught of sensation, how could she know which were her true feelings?

Over the preceding days, the abrupt changes in her opinion of him had been dizzying. She knew some of her opinions about William had been wrong, but perhaps some had been correct. He was charming now, but would he revert to cold and distant once he had won her hand? And if she agreed at this moment, would he believe it was gratitude for the gift of the ring?

Elizabeth's stomach churned queasily. How would she sort through these contradictory feelings? How could she discern which were real?

William watched her expectantly. "I cannot yet give you an answer," she murmured into his neck.

He sighed, his shoulders drooping. "Well, that is not a no."

"No. I am not rejecting you."

He gave her a pained smile. "We should join the others at the table."

***

Darcy had been hoping he could announce their engagement at Christmas dinner, but he also feared that he had pushed Elizabeth too hard and too fast. This was not a matter in which he could afford to appear high-handed.

He ground his teeth as they joined the rest of the party at the dining table. Courting Elizabeth had strained all his patience, and the master of Pemberley was not accustomed to waiting for what he wanted. Darcy took a deep breath, reminding himself that she was worth waiting for. He would simply have to dig deeper and find even more stores of patience…somewhere.

The dining table was ablaze with candles, and more illumination shone from the chandelier, which was adorned with mistletoe. The table almost groaned under the weight of the food: potatoes, leeks, mince pie, jellies, turkey, mutton, venison, and more. Darcy's cook had outdone herself; he did not know how they would eat even a fraction of it.

After prayers of thankfulness, Darcy led his guests in a toast to the festivities of the Christmas season. He was heartened by the expressions on the faces around the table. Although Mr. Bennet still regarded Darcy cautiously, his eyes no longer narrowed suspiciously at every one of his utterances. And the Gardiners seemed disposed to rather like their host. The children—who were eating their dinner in the nursery—appeared to be having a wonderful time, and Georgiana loved seeing them.

Conversation at dinner was convivial. The game of charades had eased some of the formality among relative strangers. The Darcys, Bennets, and Gardiners—as well as one Fitzwilliam— were talking with great animation. Darcy rarely hosted dinners at his house, and it was almost always for close relatives. Not naturally of a sociable disposition, he had never before hosted a big Christmas gathering. But the experience was unexpectedly enjoyable, and he found himself hoping for another such gathering. Darcy allowed his mind to wander, imagining future Christmases with Elizabeth by his side—perhaps with their own little ones receiving presents and sitting in Aunt Georgiana's lap.

Hopefully nobody noticed his little sigh of pleasure.

Hopefully Elizabeth would accept his proposal so that future might become a reality.

Darcy was startled from his reverie by a knock at the front door. Who could possibly be arriving at this hour—on Christmas day? Conversation around the table died down as everyone looked around in puzzlement.

Finally, Bates, the butler, entered the room. His face was a blank mask, but Darcy knew him well enough to recognize disapproval. "Miss Bingley is here, sir," he announced.

"Miss Bingley?" Darcy's voice actually squeaked in surprise.

"She said you invited her family for Christmas dinner, but she is the only one who could attend."

Damnation! She was presuming on the long-ago invitation. "I had invited the Bingleys, but with Mr. Bingley out of town, I assumed they had made other arrangements." More the fool he. Arriving alone and without confirming the invitation was highly irregular. But, of course, Caroline Bingley would take any opportunity to presume upon their friendship. Now that she was at Darcy House, he could not turn her away without appearing churlish.

Darcy nodded to Bates. "Please show her in and have Hillerman set another place at the table." Fortunately, the table seated twenty people easily. *If only I could have Hillerman put her all the way at the other end…*

Miss Bingley swept into the room triumphantly, a vision in orange satin with red feathers adorning her hair. Everyone stood to acknowledge her; bows and curtsies were exchanged.

She surveyed the assembled guests with disdain but evinced no surprise at the guest list. Somehow she had known who would be attending dinner at Darcy House. What was her game? "A thousand apologies for my tardiness!" she trilled as she sat. "It was very clever of you to start without me, or the food might have grown cold."

A headache—the same headache Miss Bingley always provoked—began to form at the back of Darcy's neck. Hillerman served Miss Bingley. As she ate, a somewhat stilted conversation resumed. At the head of the table, Darcy was far enough from Miss Bingley that he could not hear what she said. Her conversation was rarely worth hearing, but he worried she might spew vitriol at Elizabeth.

During a lull in the conversation, Miss Bingley directed her words to Darcy. "It is very good of you to invite the Bennet family for dinner." Her voice dripped with condescension as if the Bennets were foundlings from an orphan home whom Darcy had taken in for the night.

Darcy did not know how to respond to such an odd compliment, so he said nothing.

"I would not have expected it of you," she continued after a pause.

"Why not?" Darcy arched a brow at her.

She shrugged, spearing a potato on her fork, affecting unconcern. "You expressed such distress about the family when Charles was in Netherfield. Why, you were the one who convinced him of the desirability of separating himself from the family! I would not have expected you to seek out such a connection."

Darcy had fallen neatly into her trap.

It did not matter that she exaggerated his role in their removal from Netherfield. The substance of the accusation was correct. Never before had Darcy harbored quite so many regrets about the man he had been in Hertfordshire.

Everyone stared at Darcy, dumbfounded. Bennet's face was turning red, as if he would explode at any moment, while all color had drained from Elizabeth's face. "*You* convinced Mr. Bingley to leave Hertfordshire and abandon Jane?" she asked.

What could he possibly say?

Chapter Fourteen

William stared at Elizabeth, ashen-faced. "Yes..." he said slowly. "Mrs. Hurst, Miss Bingley, and I all spoke with Bingley about—"

"You are responsible for separating Jane from the man she loved?" Elizabeth's father was on his feet, eying William with horror.

"She seemed so..." William hesitated. "I did not think her feelings were engaged."

Elizabeth shot to her feet as well. "And why should *you* make such a determination?"

William was standing, but he kept his eyes fixed on the table. "It was not well done of me. I know it now, and I am so very sorry."

Elizabeth stood behind her chair, grabbing the back to steady herself. Her entire body shook with anger and flushed with a heat that had nothing to do with the blazing fire in the fireplace. *Perhaps I should simply leave. Papa would come with me. We could hail a cab—if they have them on Christmas Day. Or we can walk. How can I remain here? Knowing what he did, how can I stay and make polite conversation with him?*

William's obvious distress did little to mitigate Elizabeth's anger. He might regret his actions, but Jane's happiness was still ruined. Elizabeth squeezed the back of the chair until her knuckles turned white.

It took a moment to notice that many of the dinner guests were staring at her. Why?

Oh.

Oh.

In her rage Elizabeth had forgotten that William was the man who had asked her to marry him. The man whose proposal she had been on the verge of accepting under the mistletoe not half an hour earlier. Now she could not. She should not accept William's hand. She should not *wish* to accept William's hand.

And yet, somehow, she did. She wanted to marry him with a greater ferocity than she had ever wanted anything before. Her desire should have been quenched forever, yet it blazed even more heartily.

It made no sense. She was angry; that rage should drive out any other emotions, even love.

Love.

Elizabeth's breath caught. *Oh, merciful heavens, I am in love with him.*

What a terrible time to realize it.

In a flash Elizabeth understood why she had been uncomfortable accepting William's proposal. Earlier, she had not been sure she loved him, and she had been unable to imagine marrying him without love. Now she *knew* she loved him, and it did her no good.

She wanted to accept his proposal immediately. She wanted to stand on her chair and cry her acceptance to the whole room. She wanted...to kiss him before all his Christmas guests. And now was the moment when she could not.

Elizabeth's anger at William had transformed into a cold fury aimed at Miss Bingley, who had forced this unwelcome knowledge upon Elizabeth and her father. No doubt she hoped it would separate Elizabeth from William. Elizabeth had no desire to see the other woman's scheme succeed, but how could she agree to marry William after this awful revelation?

William was stricken. "Elizabeth, I did realize, and I—"

"I believe," Miss Bingley drawled, "that you had best exert your energy toward explaining why you wish to marry Elizabeth Bennet when you believed her family was not good enough for my brother?"

"I would like an answer to that question as well," Elizabeth's father said, glaring at William.

"I was wrong. I realized it not long ago." He spoke to everyone, but his eyes were fixed on Elizabeth, beseeching her. "I pray you understand. I attempted to make amends by—"

The door to the dining room opened once more, and the butler entered.

"What is it now, Bates?" William asked.

"I beg your pardon, sir, but Mr. Bingley has just arrived." Bates must have worked for years to perfect that bland non-expression.

"Charles? Here?" Miss Bingley cried. "But I did not expect him back for two more days!"

Elizabeth understood that panicked tone. No doubt her brother would be less than impressed by how Miss Bingley had insinuated herself into the Darcy House Christmas celebration and endeavored to stoke controversy. She obviously had not intended him to know until all the damage was done.

"Please show him in, Bates," William said with an air of weary resignation. At this point he would probably be happiest if all his guests departed immediately.

"Elizabeth," William said after Bates departed, "I have been trying to tell you that—"

"She accepted!" Mr. Bingley's voice preceded him into the room. "She accepted, Darcy!" The door burst open, and the man himself entered, sporting an enormous grin. "I am an engaged man."

Oh no. Elizabeth's heart froze. He had proposed to another woman already? It would break Jane's heart, and then Elizabeth could never accept William.

Mr. Bingley stopped short at the threshold, nearly tripping over himself when he realized the size of the gathering he had interrupted.

"I beg your pardon!" he exclaimed with a chagrined smile. "I apologize for intruding like this."

"Who accepted your offer, Mr. Bingley?" Elizabeth's father said in a dangerously low voice. "To whom are you engaged?"

Mr. Bingley's smile faded somewhat, and he cleared his throat. "Well...actually, sir. I have just returned from...Netherfield. While there I made a trip to Longbourn where I spoke to Jane—Miss Jane Bennet."

Elizabeth started smiling.

Miss Bingley started scowling.

"She graciously accepted my apology and my offer to love and cherish her for the rest of my life." Despite the disconcerting experience of facing Jane's father unexpectedly, Mr. Bingley glowed with happiness. "I just arrived in London today in the hopes of seeking you out to obtain your permission." He grinned despite his uncertainty. "You have saved me the trouble of a trip to Gracechurch Street, sir."

"You proposed marriage to Jane, and she accepted you?" Elizabeth's father said slowly.

Mr. Bingley smiled. "Yes, sir."

"But it was my understanding that your sister and Mr. Darcy convinced you to quit Netherfield because they felt Jane was not good enough for you," he said.

Mr. Bingley's eyes darted nervously to William and back to her father. "They did suggest it, yes, sir. But I made my own decision. Caroline and Darcy were convinced that Jane was indifferent to my attentions. However, a few days ago, Darcy visited Bingley House and said he believed he had been wrong about Jane's indifference. He encouraged me to seek her out. I left for Hertfordshire immediately for the sole purpose of ascertaining her feelings."

Miss Bingley had shrunk back into her chair, as if hoping nobody would notice her. *She* had known where her brother had traveled and with what purpose, and yet…

But Elizabeth did not have enough room in her heart for anger at that moment. She turned to William. "You told him that?"

He nodded, still regarding her warily. "I wished to make amends. The fault was mine, so should the remedy be."

"Oh, thank you!" In her haste to reach William, Elizabeth knocked over her chair, reaching the head of the table within seconds. She threw her arms around an astonished William, pulling his head down toward hers and kissing him thoroughly.

"Miss Bennet!" Mr. Bingley exclaimed in astonishment.

It was not a short kiss, either. It was deep and searching and passionate. William tightened his hold around her waist as Elizabeth snuggled in to his body. She could not bear to release him, depriving herself of his warmth. The kiss continued…

Her father loudly cleared his throat—twice. Miss Bingley sniffed her disapproval. Miss Darcy giggled.

"Ah, Darcy, perhaps there was something you neglected to mention to me?" Mr. Bingley's voice was amused.

Elizabeth did not want the kiss to end, but she had something she needed to say. Their lips parted, but she did not release her grip on his arms. "Yes," she said, holding his gaze steadily.

"Yes?" His brows drew together.

"Yes, Mr. Darcy, I will marry you."

A broad grin spread across his face. "You were wrong, Elizabeth," he said.

"About what?"

"You said you had not brought me a gift for Christmas, but you have given me the best one of all."

Epilogue

The dining room at Darcy House was very large, but it may never have hosted so many people before. The Bennets were visiting from Hertfordshire, and various Fitzwilliam relatives had arrived from Derbyshire. A number of Bingley's friends and relatives were gathered around the table as well. The children were being served their food in the breakfast room. Darcy had been hearing laughter from that direction intermittently.

"Twelfth Night is a very auspicious day for a wedding, er, weddings!" Darcy's new mother-in-law exclaimed loudly to the entire table of guests. Everyone nodded in agreement. It was at least the third time she had said the same thing; perhaps she had consumed a little too much of the wassail.

Mr. Bennet cajoled his wife back into her seat and poured her a cup of coffee. Now she was teary-eyed. "Two daughters married!" she exclaimed through her sobs. "And to such good men. We are blessed, Mr. Bennet."

"Yes, we are, my dear," he said in a low voice. "Please drink your coffee."

Darcy glanced at his new wife, who rolled her eyes with a tolerant smile. Darcy smiled, too. He was far too happy today to allow Mrs. Bennet's antics to annoy him. At the other end of the long table, Jane and Bingley—dressed in their wedding finery—were cooing at each other, oblivious to everyone around them.

Following his stare, Elizabeth laughed. "You would think they could stop gazing into each other's eyes long enough to speak with a few guests at their own wedding breakfast."

"I think Bingley believes he needs to make amends," Darcy observed.

It was true that the other couple had been inseparable since they had been reunited. Richard had observed that their hasty marriage was a blessing, or they might anticipate their vows. Jane had blushed at the suggestion, and Bingley had dismissed it, but Darcy agreed with his cousin. Of course, only he and Elizabeth knew how dangerously close they were to anticipating *their* vows. The quick wedding had not been *Bingley's* idea.

Darcy took his new wife's hand and kissed it. "Have I told you that you are the most beautiful woman here today?"

"Yes," she said with a laugh.

"Have I told you how lovely you look in your wedding gown?"

"Yes."

"Have I told you I am eager for all the guests to depart so I may have you all to myself?"

"Mr. Darcy!" Elizabeth exclaimed in mock outrage.

Whatever rejoinder Darcy would have made was cut short when Mary Bennet rushed up to their seats. "I cannot find Lydia anywhere," she said in a low tone.

Elizabeth sighed. Darcy could just imagine what kind of trouble Lydia could cause wandering loose in Darcy House, but he refused to allow it to spoil his good mood.

"Have you checked for any missing soldiers?" Elizabeth asked with a grin. "If there is a red coat nearby, she will be nearby."

Darcy glanced about for Richard, but his cousin was sitting with his parents halfway down the table. Good. The last thing the man needed was to get entangled with Lydia.

"That is why I worry," Mary replied. "Kitty swears she saw Mr. Wickham lurking about in the back hallway, but I did not think you would invite him."

Now Darcy was alarmed. "Wickham? What would bring him here?" *Nothing good.*

Elizabeth clutched his arm. "We had better find Lydia before he causes more trouble."

"Indeed," Darcy growled, hurrying to his feet. He could handle Wickham, but it would be good to have help. Darcy caught Richard's eye and nodded toward the door. Richard caught up with them in the hallway. Mary had fetched Mr. Bennet, apparently on the dubious premise that he might be of some help with Lydia.

Darcy explained the situation to everyone in low voices as they ventured into the front hallway. Richard grinned at the idea that he might have a chance to strike Wickham, but Mr. Bennet's face was grave.

They did not have far to go. The group turned the corner and found Lydia—red-faced and teary-eyed—standing outside the door of the yellow drawing room. Elizabeth rushed up to her sister. "Lydia, what has occurred?"

"They told me to leave the room!" she wailed. "They said I was too young to hear."

Elizabeth peered into her sister's face. "Who did? Hear what?"

Lydia mopped her tears with the handkerchief Elizabeth handed her. "Mr. Wickham and M-Miss Bingley!" she sobbed. "They are in the drawing room talking, and they made me leave—and told me they would pay me not to tell anyone. But W-Wickham is in there with h-her—" She crossed her arms angrily, resembling a mature adult for a moment, before bursting into tears once more.

What was Miss Bingley doing with Wickham in the drawing room? How was she even familiar with the man? Darcy could not imagine. "Please return to the dining room and fetch Bingley," he whispered in Mary's ear. She nodded once and rushed away.

"What were they discussing?" Elizabeth asked Lydia.

"I do not know!" the girl wailed. Finally, Mr. Bennet stepped forward and drew his daughter to the side, trying awkwardly to comfort her.

Darcy and Richard joined Elizabeth at the closed door of the drawing room. "What could they possibly be doing?" Richard asked. Everyone exchanged puzzled glances.

Darcy was tempted to wash his hands of it. Miss Bingley had attempted to sabotage his relationship with Elizabeth; he would never have invited her today but could not have barred her from her own brother's wedding. However, he could not ignore Wickham's disturbing presence; he should not be in the house at all. No. Darcy sighed. They must discover what occurred in the yellow drawing room.

Bingley hurried up to them, trailed by Mary. "Caroline is closeted with Wickham?" he said hoarsely. "Why?"

Darcy shook his head. "I do not know, but I believe we must discover the truth."

They could hear nothing but the murmur of voices through the thick wooden door, so Darcy eased it open just a crack. Fortunately, the hinges were well-oiled and did not creak.

"I will not pay you one more penny!" Miss Bingley screeched.

"I fulfilled my side of the bargain," Wickham insisted. "I was engaged to Elizabeth Bennet."

"For ten minutes!" Miss Bingley snapped. "It hardly signifies, and you have been amply rewarded for your pathetic efforts."

Elizabeth and Darcy exchanged looks of alarm. Wickham had been paid to propose to her? But as Darcy considered the events of the previous weeks, a number of Wickham's odd choices made more sense.

"I do not believe you thoroughly grasp the situation." Wickham's voice had turned silky. "It would be a shame if anyone found out what you paid me to do…"

Miss Bingley gasped. "That-That is blackmail!"

Beside Darcy, Bingley shook his head at his sister's stupidity.

"Oh, dear me!" Wickham exclaimed in mock outrage. "Who do you think I am? You paid me to seduce a woman! You are not dealing with the Archbishop of Canterbury here."

"Why, you—!" Miss Bingley screeched. Then there were sounds of a scuffle. Had she struck Wickham? Had he struck her? Darcy did not want her to come to harm.

He threw open the door, and all the listeners piled into the room. Darcy gasped at the sight that greeted them. Miss Bingley was sprawled on the floor, writhing under Wickham, who grinned as he pressed her hands to the carpet—preventing her from striking him.

"Caroline!" Bingley cried in alarm.

"Wickham!" Richard shouted.

The struggles stopped as both participants stared dumbfounded at the new arrivals. "I—We—Just—" Wickham babbled.

"He and I—We needed to—Remove yourself from my person!" Miss Bingley pushed ineffectively at Wickham, who appeared to rather enjoy his current position.

Other wedding guests, attracted by the commotion, were crowding the doorway. Darcy saw his aunt and uncle, Mr. Hurst, and Mr. Gardiner all watching curiously. Well, there was no hope of keeping this quiet.

Elizabeth must have reached the same conclusion. "Really!" she exclaimed. "If you wanted an assignation, did it have to occur during our wedding breakfast?"

Both Wickham and Miss Bingley gaped in horror before babbling denials: this was not an assignation, they were not doing anything illicit, this was merely a…

Unfortunately for them, their awkward situation rather belied any assertions of innocence. Wickham scrambled into a standing position, but everyone had seen him lying on top of Miss Bingley.

Finally, Darcy silenced the hubbub with a loud clearing of his throat. "If you were not meeting for an assignation," he asked, "how did you come to be in my drawing room?"

They looked sidelong at each other but were unable to think of a response. The truth would be even worse than the lie Elizabeth had promoted.

Bingley trudged over to his sister and helped her to her feet. She brushed off her rumpled clothing indignantly and righted her be-feathered hat. Bingley turned to Wickham with a deep sigh. "I hope you are prepared to do the right thing."

Wickham turned green. Miss Bingley cried, "No!" From her expression Bingley might as well have demanded she eat a plate of worms.

Bingley gave his sister an apologetic look. "Caroline, you have been compromised. You cannot marry anyone else." Then he clapped Wickham on the shoulder. "Congratulations, man. She has a good dowry." Wickham brightened momentarily but soured again at the sight of Miss Bingley's expression.

"Charles, you cannot do this!" Miss Bingley shrieked.

"I have no choice," Bingley said patiently.

Elizabeth and Darcy ushered people out of the room. This was a matter to be settled among Wickham, Bingley, and his sister. They hardly needed an audience.

One of the last people to leave the room was Mrs. Bennet, still a little tipsy. "There will be another wedding?" she exclaimed. "How wonderful! Christmastide is the time for them, you know."

As the room emptied, Bingley spoke to his sister in low tones. She trembled with anger but nodded with great reluctance.

Finally, Bingley gave Wickham a meaningful look. The man cleared his throat and approached Miss Bingley without meeting her eyes. "Miss Bingley, would you do me the honor of—?"

"Yes," she snapped before he had finished and flounced out of the room. Wickham stalked out as well, noticeably turning in the opposite direction once he was in the hallway.

"They were plotting against us the whole time!" Elizabeth exclaimed. "How horrible."

"They deserve each other," Richard muttered.

Darcy shook his head slowly. "The moment the vows are uttered, Wickham will collect the dowry and board the first ship to America." He glanced at Bingley. "Even your sister does not deserve that."

"My solicitor must write the marriage articles very carefully," Bingley said. "So instead they will be shackled together in England. Poor

Caroline. But perhaps together they will learn to improve their characters." Darcy privately believed this was an overly optimistic hope.

Bingley stared out of the doorway thoughtfully. "No doubt she believed you would propose to her, if Miss Bennet—er, Mrs. Darcy— were engaged to someone else."

Darcy shuddered. "Not if she were the last woman in the world." He turned to Elizabeth. "I thank you, my darling, for rescuing me from that fate."

She laughed, a musical sound. "My pleasure. You rescued me from Mr. Wickham—twice—so it was only fair."

At that moment, Miss Bennet—er, Mrs. Bingley—appeared in the doorway. Bingley's face dissolved into smiles as she glided across the floor to join him.

"Yes," Bingley sighed. "Everything has worked out as it should."

The End

Thank you for purchasing this book. I know you have many entertainment options, and I appreciate that you spent your time with my story.

Your support makes it possible for authors like me to continue writing.

Please consider leaving a review where you purchased the book.

Reviews are a book's lifeblood.

Learn more about me and my upcoming releases:

Sign up for my newsletter Dispatches from Pemberley

Website: www.victoriakincaid.com

Twitter: VictoriaKincaid@kincaidvic

Blog: https://kincaidvictoria.wordpress.com/

Facebook: https://www.facebook.com/kincaidvictoria

About Victoria Kincaid

The author of numerous best-selling Pride and Prejudice variations, historical romance writer Victoria Kincaid has a Ph.D. in English literature and runs a small business, er, household with two children, a hyperactive dog, an overly affectionate cat, and a husband who is not threatened by Mr. Darcy. They live near Washington DC, where the inhabitants occasionally stop talking about politics long enough to complain about the traffic.

On weekdays she is a freelance writer/editor who now specializes in IT marketing (it's more interesting than it sounds). In the past, some of her more…unusual writing subjects have included space toilets, taxi services, laser gynecology, bidets, orthopedic shoes, generating energy from onions, Ferrari rental car services, and vampire face lifts (she swears she is not making any of this up). A lifelong Austen fan, Victoria has read more Jane Austen variations and sequels than she can count – and confesses to an extreme partiality for the Colin Firth version of Pride and Prejudice.

Also by Victoria Kincaid:

President Darcy

A modern adaptation of *Pride and Prejudice*

Billionaire President William Darcy has it all: wealth, good friends, and the most powerful job in the world. Despite what his friends say, he is not lonely in the White House. He's not. And he has vowed not to date while he's in office. Nor is he interested in Elizabeth Bennet. Although she is pretty and funny and smart, her family is nouveau riche and unbearable. To make it worse, he encounters her everywhere in Washington D.C.—making it harder and harder to ignore her. Why can't he get Elizabeth Bennet out of his mind?

Elizabeth Bennet enjoys her job with the Red Cross and loves her family, despite their tendency to embarrass themselves. When they drag her to a White House state dinner, they cause her to make a unfavorable impression on the president, who labels her unattractive and uninteresting—words that are immediately broadcast on Twitter. Now the whole world knows the president dissed her. All Elizabeth wants is to avoid the man—who, let's admit it, is proud and difficult. For some reason he acts so friendly when they keep running into each other, but she just knows he's judging her.

Eventually circumstances force Darcy and Elizabeth to confront their true feelings for each other, with explosive results. But even if they can find common ground, Darcy is still the president—with limited privacy and unlimited responsibilities—and his enemies won't hesitate to use his feelings for Elizabeth to hurt his presidency.

Can President Darcy and Elizabeth Bennet find their way to happily ever after?

Darcy vs. Bennet

Elizabeth Bennet is drawn to a handsome, mysterious man she meets at a masquerade ball. However, she gives up all hope for a future with him when she learns he is the son of George Darcy, the man who ruined her father's life. Despite her father's demand that she avoid the younger Darcy, when he appears in Hertfordshire Elizabeth cannot stop thinking about him, or seeking him out, or welcoming his kisses....

Fitzwilliam Darcy has struggled to carve out a life independent from his father's vindictive temperament and domineering ways, although the elder Darcy still controls the purse strings. After meeting Elizabeth Bennet, Darcy cannot imagine marrying anyone else, even though his father despises her family. More than anything he wants to make her his wife, but doing so would mean sacrificing everything else....

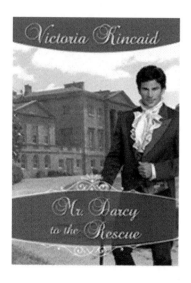

Mr. Darcy to the Rescue

When the irritating Mr. Collins proposes marriage, Elizabeth Bennet is prepared to refuse him, but then she learns that her father is ill. If Mr. Bennet dies, Collins will inherit Longbourn and her family will have nowhere to go. Elizabeth accepts the proposal, telling herself she can be content as long as her family is secure. If only she weren't dreading the approaching wedding day…

Ever since leaving Hertfordshire, Mr. Darcy has been trying to forget his inconvenient attraction to Elizabeth. News of her betrothal forces him to realize how devastating it would be to lose her. He arrives at Longbourn intending to prevent the marriage, but discovers Elizabeth's real opinion about his character. Then Darcy recognizes his true dilemma…

How can he rescue her when she doesn't want him to?

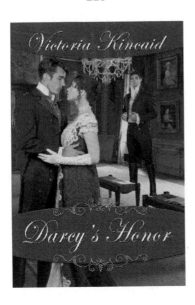

Darcy's Honor

Elizabeth Bennet is relieved when the difficult Mr. Darcy leaves the area after the Netherfield Ball. But she soon runs afoul of Lord Henry, a Viscount who thinks to force her into marrying him by slandering her name and ruining her reputation. An outcast in Meryton, and even within her own family, Elizabeth has nobody to turn to and nowhere to go.

Darcy successfully resisted Elizabeth's charms during his visit to Hertfordshire, but when he learns of her imminent ruin, he decides he must propose to save her from disaster. However, Elizabeth is reluctant to tarnish Darcy's name by association…and the viscount still wants her…

Can Darcy save his honor while also marrying the woman he loves?

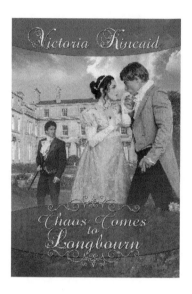

Chaos Comes to Longbourn

While attempting to suppress his desire to dance with Elizabeth Bennet, Mr. Darcy flees the Netherfield ballroom only to stumble upon a half-dressed Lydia Bennet in the library. When they are discovered in this compromising position by a shrieking Mrs. Bennet, it triggers a humorously improbable series of events. After the dust settles, eight of Jane Austen's characters are engaged to the wrong person.

Although Darcy yearns for Elizabeth, and she has developed feelings for the master of Pemberley, they are bound by promises to others. How can Darcy and Elizabeth unravel this tangle of hilariously misbegotten betrothals and reach their happily ever after?

Pride and Proposals

What if Mr. Darcy's proposal was too late?

Darcy has been bewitched by Elizabeth Bennet since he met her in Hertfordshire. He can no longer fight this overwhelming attraction and must admit he is hopelessly in love. During Elizabeth's visit to Kent she has been forced to endure the company of the difficult and disapproving Mr. Darcy, but she has enjoyed making the acquaintance of his affable cousin, Colonel Fitzwilliam.

Finally resolved, Darcy arrives at Hunsford Parsonage prepared to propose—only to discover that Elizabeth has just accepted a proposal from the Colonel, Darcy's dearest friend in the world. As he watches the couple prepare for a lifetime together, Darcy vows never to speak of what is in his heart. Elizabeth has reason to dislike Darcy, but finds that he haunts her thoughts and stirs her emotions in strange ways.

Can Darcy and Elizabeth find their happily ever after?

The Secrets of Darcy and Elizabeth

A despondent Darcy travels to Paris in the hopes of forgetting the disastrous proposal at Hunsford. Paris is teeming with English visitors during a brief moment of peace in the Napoleonic Wars, but Darcy's spirits don't lift until he attends a ball and unexpectedly encounters…Elizabeth Bennet! Darcy seizes the opportunity to correct misunderstandings and initiate a courtship.

Their moment of peace is interrupted by the news that England has again declared war on France, and hundreds of English travelers must flee Paris immediately. Circumstances force Darcy and Elizabeth to escape on their own, despite the risk to her reputation. Even as they face dangers from street gangs and French soldiers, romantic feelings blossom during their flight to the coast. But then Elizabeth falls ill, and the French are arresting all the English men they can find….

When Elizabeth and Darcy finally return to England, their relationship has changed, and they face new crises. However, they have secrets they must conceal—even from their own families.

When Mary Met the Colonel

Without the beauty and wit of the older Bennet sisters or the liveliness of the younger, Mary is the Bennet sister most often overlooked. She has resigned herself to a life of loneliness, alleviated only by music and the occasional book of military history.

Colonel Fitzwilliam finds himself envying his friends who are marrying wonderful women while he only attracts empty-headed flirts. He longs for a caring, well-informed woman who will see the man beneath the uniform.

A chance meeting in Longbourn's garden during Darcy and Elizabeth's wedding breakfast kindles an attraction between Mary and the Colonel. However, the Colonel cannot act on these feelings since he must wed an heiress. He returns to war, although Mary finds she cannot easily forget him.

Is happily ever after possible when Mary meets the Colonel?

A Very Darcy Christmas

A *Pride and Prejudice* sequel. Elizabeth and Darcy are preparing for their first Christmas at Pemberley when they are suddenly deluged by a flood of uninvited guests. Mrs. Bennet is seeking refuge from the French invasion she believes to be imminent. Lady Catherine brings two suitors for Georgiana's hand, who cause a bit of mayhem themselves. Lydia's presence causes bickering—and a couple of small fires—while Wickham has more nefarious plans in mind....The abundance of guests soon puts a strain on her marriage as Elizabeth tries to manage the comedy and chaos while ensuring a happy Christmas for all.

Meanwhile, Georgiana is finding her suitors—and the prospect of coming out—to be very unappealing. Colonel Fitzwilliam seems to be the only person who understands her fondness for riding astride and shooting pistols. Georgiana realizes she's beginning to have more than cousinly feelings for him, but does he return them? And what kind of secrets is he hiding?

Love, romance, and humor abound as everyone gathers to celebrate a Very Darcy Christmas.

Made in the USA
Columbia, SC
11 April 2019